THE FIRST
SHALL BE LAST

A Sharyn Howard Mystery

Other books by Joyce and Jim Lavene:

The *Sharyn Howard Mystery* Series

Last Dance
One Last Good-bye
The Last to Remember
Until Our Last Embrace
For the Last Time
Dreams Don't Last
Last Fires Burning
Glory's Last Victim
Last Rites
Last One Down
Before the Last Lap

Also Writing as Joyce Ames:

A Time for Love
If Not for You
Only You
Save Your Heart for Me
The Dowager Duchess
Madison's Miracles

THE FIRST SHALL BE LAST

•

Joyce and Jim Lavene

AVALON BOOKS
NEW YORK

Lav

Published by Thomas Bouregy & Co., Inc.
160 Madison Avenue, New York, NY 10016

Library of Congress Cataloging-in-Publication Data

Lavene, Joyce.
    The first shall be last : a Sharyn Howard mystery / Joyce and
Jim Lavene.
        p. cm.
    ISBN 978-0-8034-9838-9 (acid-free paper)
    I. Lavene, James.   II. Title.

PS3562.A8479F57 2007
813'.6—dc22

                                                2007008133

PRINTED IN THE UNITED STATES OF AMERICA
ON ACID-FREE PAPER
BY HADDON CRAFTSMEN, BLOOMSBURG, PENNSYLVANIA

For Erin, who has seen us through most of Sharyn's books with wit and understanding, and Mayor Tom Garrison of Badin who believed in his hometown that we have come to love so much.

Prologue

Sheriff Sharyn Howard looked down at the grave after the mourners and the burial crew were gone. A brisk wind blew off of Diamond Mountain scattering the autumn leaves around her feet, a portent of the winter to come.

The granite grave marker that would honor the fallen Diamond Springs police officer buried here wasn't ready yet. Every man and woman in the county had donated for it. She'd seen Bobby Bradley working on the chunk of cold gray stone.

Officer David Matthews died in the performance of his duties. He died a man of honor and valor.

1

She still found it hard to believe David was gone. They'd graduated high school together. He'd been her deputy for years before he joined the town's police force. During that time he was everything from a thorn in her side to a pain in her neck. She'd been happy to see him go to the new police department. She would never forget him telling her he wanted her to be proud of him as he lay dying.

He didn't deserve to die. She felt responsible. It was partly her investigation into the good-old-boy network that ran Montgomery County and Diamond Springs, and partly slipshod work from the FBI that got him killed.

She heard footsteps approaching and glanced up, the wind tugging at her flat-brimmed sheriff's hat. "What do *you* want?"

FBI Agent Brewster, the man she blamed more than herself for David's death, looked out over the patchwork quilt of fall color that lay sprawled beneath the mountain. In the heart of it was Diamond Lake, sparkling like a sapphire in the sun. "Sheriff, I know a way we can get these men. Are you game?"

After David's death, after everything that had happened, she knew she should say no. But her heart wanted vengeance. "What do you have in mind?"

Chapter One

The Montgomery County North Carolina Sheriff's Department had its hands full with bad weather and worse roads. An ice storm had crippled the county, leaving most people without basic services. Despite warnings on television and radio, drivers insisted on going out. The result was piles of crushed metal and injuries that were difficult to get to the hospital in Diamond Springs.

"We've got an ambulance in a ditch," head deputy Ernie Watkins said. "That makes two this morning."

"It won't get any better until the roads clear." Deputy Ed Robinson put on his heavy, sheepskin jacket. "I hate to go out there without a Hummer."

"I'll just request that for you," his wife, Trudy, replied with a laugh. "I'm sure they'll jump right on it."

"Where's Sharyn?" Ed asked. "I could at least take her Jeep."

Ernie sighed. "Wherever she takes herself off to nowadays."

Before Ed could comment, the door to the makeshift sheriff's office blew open with a cold gust of wind. It had a habit of doing that. Like everything else down there, it was falling apart.

The new sheriff's office was scheduled to be completed in the fall, but fall seemed a long way off at that moment. The basement of the courthouse was cold and damp but it was the best the county commission said they could do until the new building was completed. None of the deputies could help thinking about their old building that now housed the Diamond Springs Police Department.

Sheriff Sharyn Howard, bundled up in a dark brown wool coat, hat, and gloves, strode in with the wind and snow that swirled for a moment before it settled. She pushed the warped door closed behind her, kicking it in place for good measure.

Sharyn was the third generation of law enforcement in Montgomery County, the first woman ever to be elected as sheriff in North Carolina. She followed her grandfather, Jacob Howard, who was the first sheriff elected in Montgomery County and her father, T. Raymond Howard, who was killed in a convenience store robbery one quiet Sunday morning.

She was tall for a woman, an even six feet, and broad-shouldered. She wore her brown sheriff's uniform and her grandfather's World War Two service revolver with a dignity and poise that was hard won over the last three years as sheriff.

She'd lost weight during the year, baby fat she called it, but she would never be of runway model proportions. Her uniform, designed for a man, showed her wide hips and large bosom to disadvantage and the drab color did nothing for her ruddy complexion.

At the age of 30, she had been reelected as sheriff despite a tough race against an experienced opponent. It gave her confidence she didn't have before. She took off her knitted cap, the one her Aunt Selma made, and shook her copper-red curls free. "What a mess!"

"Where have you been?" Trudy asked. "We were looking for you everywhere."

"I had to meet with three commissioners this morning. That's all that could make it in, but that gives them a quorum to make decisions. They've decided not to hire a temp to take Joe's place while he's in Afghanistan. We're going to be short-handed for however long it takes."

Longtime deputy Joe Landers had left for a Middle East assignment with his reserve unit in late fall. They'd had less than 24 hours warning that he was going and no idea when he'd be back.

"We've handled the whole county with fewer hands

than we have now," Ernie reminded her. "I think we can manage."

It had been only a short time since the county decided to create a police department for Diamond Springs, leaving the sheriff's department to take care of the rest of the county. The area had grown rapidly with the new interstate highway that sliced through the area. It brought jobs, residents, and badly needed tax dollars. But it also brought more crime and changes none of them expected.

Montgomery County was crisscrossed by the Uwharrie Mountains, three rivers, one-lane highways, and old bridges. The loss of one deputy, especially on a day like this, was deeply felt.

"That's true," Ed agreed, his baby blue eyes, curly blond hair, and year-round tan making him appear younger than his fifty-something years. "We'll manage."

"We always do." Ernie smiled his crooked smile as he handed Sharyn her mail.

Another blast of cold wind accompanied Deputies Marvella Honeycutt and JP Santiago into the office. They stamped snow from their boots and rubbed their hands together as they shivered in the basement.

"Where's Terry?" Sharyn noticed their newest deputy was missing.

"He's out with a tow truck driver trying to get an eighteen-wheeler off the road. The driver skidded halfway down the mountain and ended up sideways across the highway." Trudy, pencil perpetually stuck in her mousy brown hair, answered the phone after she explained.

"There's another ambulance in a ditch," Ed told Sharyn. "The highway patrol can't handle all of it. They want us to come out and help."

"Okay. Take my Jeep." She tossed him the keys. "But be careful."

"I was hoping you'd say that." He rubbed his hands together then put on his gloves.

"It's awful out there," Marvella told them. "Maybe we should just wait to send anyone else out until it's over. We can't help if we're all in the ditch!"

"I've got a fatality." Trudy hung up the emergency phone. "Car versus pedestrian."

Sharyn groaned. "Where at?"

"Out in Frog Meadow."

"We can do that for you, Sheriff." JP nudged Marvella. "No need for you to go out in the bad weather."

"Thanks, JP. But I think I can handle it."

"No, really," Marvella insisted. "It's not that bad out there. We'll take it."

"The law says the sheriff has to be at the scene of a fatality in the county," Ernie quoted. "No getting away from it."

"You and Marvella stay here and warm up. Don't go out unless you have to," Sharyn instructed. "Ernie and I will take care of this. Trudy, see if you can find us someone who'd like to lend us a few four-wheel-drive vehicles. And get some help answering that phone!"

Sharyn put her hat and gloves back on, taking the address of the pedestrian accident from Trudy. "Let us know if anything else comes up. JP, try to get in touch with the National Weather Service and find out how long this is supposed to last."

"Yes, ma'am!"

Ernie and Sharyn trudged out into the snow behind Ed. The sky was as white with thick, fat flakes as the ground leading up to it. There was no way to tell where one ended and the other began.

"At least Joe is warm in Afghanistan." Ernie shivered despite his heavy brown jacket.

"Too warm according to his emails," Sharyn said. "Maybe we can send him some of this."

"I assume we're taking my truck?"

"You got it. What's the good of having a four-wheel-drive truck if you don't drive it in the snow?"

"I *could* make the case that it's not a department vehicle." He used his keyless entry to open the doors to his new red GM truck.

The snow crunched under Sharyn's booted feet. There was at least a foot on the ground already. If it didn't stop soon, they wouldn't be able to get out at all. "When did that ever stop anyone from taking *my* Jeep?"

Ernie got behind the wheel and the truck purred to life. "That's why you get all that extra money as sheriff."

She laughed. "Yeah, right. Just drive the truck and don't go into any ditches."

Inside, the cab was warm and dry. Sharyn unbuttoned her coat and took off her hat as she looked at the address on the paper. "1547 Eastmont. That's right there on the highway in Frog Meadow."

"Not that there's much *off* the highway in Frog Meadow," Ernie quipped, glancing at her before he started out of the parking lot to the almost invisible roads. "He's gonna be there, you know. No way around it."

"I know." She stared out the side window, not even able to see the craggy face of Diamond Mountain in the distance. "A fatality means we both have to be there. I was hoping we wouldn't have one for a few more years."

She wasn't looking forward to seeing Montgomery County Medical Examiner Nick Thomopolis. That was putting it mildly. The relationship they'd worked so hard to keep going was in pieces.

It was her fault. It had been a difficult decision to make after David Matthews' death, but she'd swallowed her pride and forced herself to pretend she was in love with Senator Jack Winter.

She was trying to find a way to trap him, to make him pay for everything he'd done. She'd tried everything else the law could provide for the last few years, but nothing had worked. She was desperate to find a way to avenge David and her father. Jack was responsible for both of their deaths.

Sharyn couldn't tell anyone the truth. Nick and her family, the men and women she worked with, all had to think it was really over between her and Nick. It was the hardest thing she'd ever done. She wasn't secretive by nature, but if it meant finally putting Jack behind bars, she could learn to keep this secret.

Jack had expressed romantic interest in her since she took office as sheriff. All she had to do was pretend to be heartbroken after her very public breakup with Nick. Jack had bought the whole story. His ego and arrogance made him an easy target.

In some ways, she was surprised Nick didn't leave Diamond Springs when they broke up. She half expected him to. He'd threatened to resign before they got together, later confessing he couldn't work with her every day and not tell her how he felt. Guilt and her own misgivings over her decision was eating her up. *How are you feeling now, Nick?*

"He'll get over it," Ernie assured her as the truck plowed through drifts mounded up by the strong wind that constantly blew down from the mountains. "You will too, I expect."

"What do you mean?"

"Don't even *try* to tell me you're happy with Jack. Nick was almost too old for you. Jack's old enough to be your father. Maybe your *grand*father. You're just on the rebound from your relationship with Nick. I know it will pass. If I didn't, I'd throw up every time I see the two of you together."

Sharyn ignored his caustic tone. "I was looking for someone different."

"You should have been looking for someone *human!*"

"Ernie!"

"All right. All right. I know when to butt out."

"*Whatever!* I hope we can *find* Frog Meadow." Sharyn changed the subject. She tried not to discuss personal matters in the office, but it was almost impossible with a group of people who'd known her since she was a child. Ernie had been like a father to her since her father, T. Raymond, was killed. There was almost nothing he didn't know about her. In turn, she knew all the ups and downs of his relationship with Annie, his high school sweetheart, who'd come back into his life a few years ago.

Growing up in a small town was bad enough with all the gossips, but the sheriff's department was like a small family all its own. She couldn't change the color of her towels without everyone knowing. Sometimes, she supposed, it was nice not having to explain things to people. Other times, like today, when she knew every eye was going to be on her and Nick, it was terrible.

Sharyn didn't let herself dwell on it as she and Ernie monitored calls between the vehicles in the field and the office. They got a call for help from the Diamond

Springs Police Department. She grabbed the radio and asked Trudy what was wrong.

"Chief Tarnower says they have a man trapped in his house in town. All of his men are out and they need assistance."

"Okay. Send Marvella and JP out to see if they can help."

"Okay, Sheriff. But they aren't gonna like it."

"Shouldn't we have some sort of code like they do in the city?" Ernie suggested when she was done talking to Trudy. "You know, like ten-four or yes, ma'am. Something that sounds a little respectful."

"You know Trudy." Sharyn yawned and closed her eyes, leaning her head back against the seat.

"Not sleeping good?"

"No. But please don't start."

"Sharyn, you know I love you like a daughter."

"Which is the preface for I'm going to give you some advice whether you want it or not."

"Exactly." Ernie carefully turned down the old back road that led to Frog Meadow, not attempting to take the interstate. "You and Nick were made for each other. You were happy together. What happened?"

Sharyn's mind went blank with the question, partly from being tired and partly because she'd trained herself to shut down when anyone mentioned Nick's name. It had only been a few months: *Sixty-four days, twelve hours, thirty-one minutes, fourteen seconds.* She wished it could be different, but no one ever said life was fair or forgiving. She did what she had to do.

"Just drive, Ernie," she muttered. "That should be enough to keep even *you* busy."

He shook his head but didn't say anything else until he saw the flashing blue lights through the snow. He stopped the truck and stared at the side of Sharyn's face when she didn't move. She was asleep, even snoring a little, her head tipped back and mouth slightly open. *What in the world was she up to?*

He was about to nudge her when a heavy rap on the window woke her and made his head shoot up. It was a highway patrol officer. Sharyn rolled down her window, snow and freezing air blowing into the warm interior of the truck.

"I'm handing this over to you, Sheriff. We got plenty of stuff goin' on down the highway." The younger man wiped snow from his ruddy face.

Sharyn yawned and nodded. "We'll take it from here, Tim. Thanks. Anything we should know?"

Officer Tim Striker shrugged. "The world is a sick place? But I expect you know that, Sheriff."

Sharyn quickly rolled up her window and stared at Ernie while she put her hat and gloves back on. "I don't think I want to know what that means."

"Me either." He pushed down the single sprig of hair on top of his head and pulled his stocking cap over it. "Let's get this over with."

The snow was piled neatly around the body lying in the street. A large pool of blood had congealed on the ground around the forlorn figure. People began to spill out of their houses to see what was going on. Even on the worst of days, everyone was curious.

A man leaning on a shovel was the logical choice for having cleaned up the scene. He was a large man with thick, brown hair and a cigarette stuck in his mouth. His dark blue plaid flannel shirt looked like it needed a washing and his unlaced boots had seen better days years before. He was talking with Megan, one of the medical examiner's assistants. But Sharyn knew Nick had to be there somewhere.

She kept looking until she saw him, dark coat and hair flecked with white snow flakes as he bent down close to the victim in the road. It was stupid, she knew, but she couldn't stop herself from looking for him. She'd seen him last week coming out of the coffee shop across from the courthouse. She'd ducked behind a gate to avoid talking to him. She was pretty sure he didn't see her.

Their courtship hadn't been easy. Nick had been surly and sarcastic and she had tried to avoid thinking about him. Deciding to break up with him to get at Jack had been even harder. Sometimes she felt like she'd fall apart if she didn't see him that day. Sometimes she wished she could run away and never see him again. *Why didn't he leave?*

She wanted him to look up and see her and she didn't ever want to look into his eyes again. It was an emotional tug-of-war that was keeping her up nights and turning her mostly logical brain to mush.

Seeing Ernie's interested gaze, she quickly averted her eyes and spoke to Keith, another one of Nick's assistants. "So what happened here?"

Chapter Two

"Looks like a woman was about to cross the road. A car came through and hit her." Keith obliged her in a prosaic way.

Sharyn glared at him. He was learning to be just like Nick.

"What?" Ernie came up behind them. "Are you saying this was deliberate?"

"That's what he's saying." Nick was careful not to look at Sharyn. "Someone decided this was a good day to practice hit and run."

"What can you tell us?" Sharyn asked gruffly, not looking any higher than Nick's shoes. She shook her head. The man refused to wear boots. He thought he was still living on the civilized blocks of New York where they plowed the streets. What was wrong with him?

She stopped herself before she thought about him catching his death of cold and totally turned into her mother.

"The man with the shovel is the neighbor, Jeet Marts. He says he found her out here when he came out to shovel snow." Nick cleared his throat, not looking up from his clipboard.

Megan butted in between them. "I'll handle this. Whatever *she* wants to know, *she* can ask me."

Sharyn knew she wasn't popular with the ME's department after she and Nick broke up but she was surprised by Megan's attitude. Well, not *really* surprised. Megan had always had a smart mouth. Maybe she was surprised because Nick let the girl talk like that. Usually . . .

But this wasn't usual. Nothing was usual anymore.

It didn't matter. Sharyn squared her shoulders and faced down the purple-haired college student. "Unless you suddenly became the county medical examiner today, I suggest you find something else to do. Maybe you could go and make a snowman."

Megan all but hissed at her.

"The sheriff is right," Nick corrected his young assistant. "I need pictures taken of the area. Get to it."

Keith pulled her away. But Megan's murderous gaze was still latched onto Sharyn's face.

"They get so attached when they're that age." Ernie shook his head. "I'll just go and talk to Mr. Marts. Maybe you two can patch things up or something before we all kill each other."

Sharyn shivered in the fierce wind that drifted the snow back over the crime scene even as they fought to keep it clear. She stared up at the sky then leveled her blue eyes to Nick's dark ones. "Do you know who the woman is?"

"Michelle Frey, twenty-two. Her purse was knocked a few feet away from her. We'll process everything and let you know what we find. But I don't think it's a straight hit and run."

"It looks like the car swerved to hit her instead of trying to miss her. Is that what you see?" Sharyn looked up the road that was mostly blocked by snow mounding as high as six feet, more where it had something to lean against.

He sighed. "It works like this. I tell you what I find. You decide what happened and charge someone. Why aren't you sleeping?"

"Nick—"

"If those circles get any bigger under your eyes, you'll look like that kid in *The Ring.*"

"*Nick!*"

"Oh. Sorry. None of my business what you and *Jack* do in your spare time."

Sharyn wanted to close her eyes and wake up somewhere else. The cold made her skin feel stretched too tight across her cheekbones. Her eyes hurt from the terrible white light. She missed the smell of spring on the mountain, that mixture of dirt and life. Spring was such a long way off. She wasn't sure she could make it through the cold this year.

"I'm sorry," Nick apologized finally.

Sharyn realized she had closed her eyes when she opened them and saw his sharply defined face: big Greek nose, soulful black eyes with those ridiculously long lashes. He looked tired too. A dark shadow seemed permanently lodged in the hollows of his cheeks. She hated that she was doing this to them. Hated that there was no other way.

"Let's start again." Nick smiled though it was clear the effort was painful. "We can at least be civil and professional."

He walked her through the crime scene, his breath frosting in the cold. "She's only been dead a few hours. The car was going pretty fast, even with the snow, to do the damage I see in her. Massive internal injuries. She bled out right here on the street."

"Is it possible whoever hit her didn't see her?"

"Possible. At least to begin with. But he or she had to notice the big bump. There was probably damage done to the vehicle. Hopefully I'll be able to isolate some paint flecks on her clothes."

Sharyn looked from the red-tinged snow to the tire

marks being filled in by the storm. "Were you able to get a cast?"

"We got it. No sign of the vehicle trying to stop. Whoever did this turned a little, pointed at her and mowed her down."

"Thanks. We'll find out what we can about Ms. Frey. Keep me posted on the autopsy and the tire marks."

"I will."

Was there something else to say? She wanted to leave yet lingered, not speaking, as she squinted off into the white distance. Nick stamped his feet and blew on his bare hands but didn't move away either. Megan and Keith processed the scene while Ernie talked to the crowd that was building up despite the weather that was getting worse.

It was the sound of the approaching ambulance that made them break away. Nick glanced up as Sharyn looked back at him. She started to speak, leaned toward him, then turned away. Nick drew in a sharp breath and walked back to his Cadillac Escalade.

"I swear I don't know what's wrong with her," Ernie commiserated under his breath as he reached him.

"Not everyone lives happily ever after." Nick shrugged. "It was good while it lasted."

"She's not happy with *him*," Ernie spat out. "I can't figure it."

Nick put his hand on the deputy's shoulder. "Don't

try. If there's a way to understand this, I don't want to know about it."

Ernie muttered beneath his breath as he approached the woman he'd known since he could toss her in the air and catch her. "Nobody saw anything. The snow was coming down too fast. They wouldn't be out here now except that we are."

"Makes sense, I suppose. Only one person needed to see her out here. The driver who killed her." Sharyn stared down at the woman's body, half covered by the gray blanket. She was pretty, even in death. Her face was clean, eyes closed like she was sleeping. "But where's her coat? It's cold out here. She's dressed up, but no coat."

"You mean like she was meeting someone out here and wanted to look pretty." Ernie wrote in his notebook. "And look at her shoes. Little bitty heels. She wasn't goin' far in those today."

"Let's find out what we can about her. Maybe what Nick can tell us will take care of the rest."

"About Nick . . ."

"Not now, Ernie," Sharyn warned. "Let's go see what we can find in Ms. Frey's house."

Ernie pointed her toward a small, yellow house that Marts had identified as the victim's home. Snow had blown on one side of it almost to the roof. A few of the green shingles were missing, but otherwise the property was in good repair. There was a pretty peacock chair and clay flower pot on the porch. A small fountain with a statue of a mermaid sat quietly in one corner.

Sharyn knocked on the door. The chances were good Ms. Frey was alone since no relative seemed to be mourning her, but it was a courtesy. When there was no answer, she opened the door and walked inside.

"What about Marts?" she asked Ernie. "He found her."

The inside of the house was pretty too. Pink-and-green-checked curtains hung at the kitchen window and frilly, feminine slipcovers were on the chairs in the small living room. The house was tiny, maybe one or two bedrooms, probably not more than eight-hundred square feet. There were plenty of these built by the old cotton mills to house their workers. When the mills closed down, the houses were sold.

"I don't know. Could be something there. He seemed about as bright as a bucket of fish, but if he was nervous or anxious, I couldn't tell it."

"I guess that would be too easy." Sharyn looked through the magazines on the table. All Martha Stewart discourses on making purses out of bananas and such.

"Sheriff," Ernie called out from a bedroom as she looked at the mail on the kitchen table.

She found him in one of the small bedrooms. A heavy feeling settled into the pit of her stomach as she saw the toys and the small bed. There were *Star Wars* posters on the walls and a kid's computer on a desk near the window. "There's a child."

Ernie picked up a photo from the desk. "Michelle and a boy. He may be three or four."

Sharyn looked around. "Where is he?"

"I hope to goodness he's at daycare or with his grandma." Ernie shook his head, running a finger along his thick mustache. "Or we've got a bigger problem than we thought."

"Let's not jump the gun," she advised. "There could be a husband too."

"Not one living here. Did you see those pink doo-dads out there? I wouldn't let Annie have something like that if I was living here."

"You'd let Annie have whatever she pleased."

"I suppose that's true. But she wouldn't do this to me."

Sharyn walked down the short hallway to the second bedroom. The bedroom was slightly bigger but even frillier than the rest of the house. Everything was pink, including netting that draped down over the bed. There were silk flowers and stuffed animals everywhere.

"This really gives it away," Ernie said when he saw it. "No man would sleep in this room."

"You might be right." Sharyn looked at one of the photos on the bedside table. "Lots of pictures of her and the boy, but none of anyone else."

Keith followed them into the house, pushing back his glasses and looking at the room. "Nick wants me to start processing in here. He thought it might be safer if he didn't send Megan in."

"Yeah, that girl must not have noticed the big Colt the sheriff wears," Ernie said. "Her grandfather shot a few men with it. The sheriff has shot a few herself."

"Don't ask me." Keith held up his hands. "I just work with her now. The woman's crazy."

"So you all broke up too?" Ernie shook his head. "I guess nobody stays together anymore."

"I think she's hot for Nick." Keith glanced at Sharyn. "Sorry, Sheriff."

"It doesn't have anything to do with me anymore." She changed the subject, her voice thick as wood. "We're going to look around a little more in here and see if we can find someone to call about the accident."

"I'll try to stay out of your way."

Sharyn went to the kitchen table and picked up the mail again. "There's an insurance document here. If nothing else, maybe Ms. Frey's agent can tell us something about her."

"What kind of insurance?" Ernie wondered.

"Car insurance." Sharyn read the document. "Ms. Frey has a blue mini van, license number two-three-seven-eight-F-R-P. We'll take this with us. Maybe we can get a hit from DMV."

"So where's her mini van?" Ernie glanced out the window. "Why wasn't she getting into that instead of walking down to the road?"

"I'm more worried about the boy." Sharyn tapped the

letter against her chin. "Let's ask Mr. Marts about him and the van and see what he has to say."

"She seemed to be walking across the street." Ernie shrugged. "Maybe the boy is over there playing or something."

"That would be nice, but why wouldn't the babysitter want to know what's going on?"

"I don't know. Maybe she's deaf."

They walked back out into the cold together. Jeet Marts was still outside dazzling his neighbors with his information about the crime. Ernie pulled him to the side of the crowd and asked him about the missing boy.

"Yeah, she has a son. Maybe two or three years old." Marts jabbed his shovel into the snow a few times and spit a big wad of brown tobacco on the ground. "He's a good kid."

"Do you know where he is?" Sharyn asked.

"He goes to a daycare, I think. Michelle is a nurse at Diamond Springs Hospital."

"Where's her van?" Ernie wondered.

"Don't know." Marts looked around. "It was there last night when she got home."

"What time was that?" Sharyn glanced around at the crowd that was alternating between watching them and trying to get a good look at the body.

"About six, like always," Marts answered. "Hey, why don't you ask his daddy? Maybe he knows. They've had some trouble on and off but maybe he's taking care of the boy."

"Does the boy have a name?" Ernie looked up from his notebook.

"Daniel. And the father's name is Jackson."

"First or last?" Sharyn asked.

"You got me. I just heard her call him Jackson."

"Thank you for your help, Mr. Marts." Ernie shook his hand. "You got a phone number where we can reach you if we have more questions?"

Marts gave him his number. "Wish I could be more help."

"We appreciate your time, Mr. Marts." Sharyn gave him her gloved hand. "If you think of anything else, please give us a call." She pulled out her cell phone as she walked away from the man.

"What are we doing?" Ernie asked.

"Calling in everyone we can find to help look for Daniel. Until we know where he is, we have to assume he's lost or possibly a kidnap victim. Every second counts."

Ernie looked around at the dwindling snowfall. "It's gonna get cold with the snow ending."

"Let's hope Daniel's not outside."

Chapter Three

Doody Franklin's dogs were the best trackers in the county, but they were busy trying to find some hikers trapped on Diamond Mountain in the snowstorm. Sharyn had no deputies available. She called Chief Tarnower who couldn't do anything to help either. All of his officers were involved in trying to maintain the city. He recommended she call in the National Guard.

She wasn't opposed to that idea, but when she made the call, the guardsmen were busy at the airport trying to dig a plane out of a snow bank. Their sergeant said they would come when they could.

"No rush or anything," Sharyn said, frustrated. "We just have a little boy trapped outside somewhere who might freeze to death overnight."

The sergeant said he understood and would send troops as soon as he could, but the surveillance plane had to take off within the hour.

Sharyn called the TV station in Diamond Springs and asked them to put out an alert for volunteers who could come out and search. She also called the State Bureau of Investigation and asked for an Amber Alert to be put out for the child. She didn't know if the boy disappeared when his mother was hit by the car or if he was a victim of foul play. Better to be safe than sorry.

In the meantime, Michelle's neighbors volunteered to help. They put on boots and coats and tramped through the mounds of snow, calling for the little boy as the wind grew sharper and plunged the temperature.

"She couldn't have been going to work," Ernie said as he and Sharyn tried to make sure volunteers were working at different places by marking their paths on a map of the area. "She wasn't dressed for it."

"Right now, I'm more worried about Daniel. There's plenty of time to figure out what happened to his mother. Nick and his team will be working on that too."

"I know. But I might as well work on the riddle in my mind. I don't like thinking about that little boy being out here all alone."

The snow had stopped and the sun was trying to creep out from behind the mountains. There were only a few hours of daylight left. The temperatures would plummet once that happened. If they couldn't find Daniel by then . . .

But where else could he be? Sharyn searched around the perimeter of the house again. There were no footprints. Nothing to show where the boy might have gone after his mother was hit by the car. If she'd been out in the road for a few hours though, everything would be covered by snow. Ernie was right. If they knew what Michelle was *doing* in the road, they might have some idea where to find Daniel.

Some cars pulled into the open area of the street. Sharyn watched as the drivers got out and talked to Ernie. He assigned a search area to each man or woman and gave each of them a walkie-talkie.

Sharyn recognized some of them. There were a few firemen and County Building Inspector, John Schmidt. Restin Lewis, night intake officer at the county jail, took a map. So did Fire Chief Dennis Wallace.

But one man caught her eye. He bypassed Ernie's checkpoint in the street and ran up to Michelle's house. Sharyn intercepted him at the front door.

"Let me through," he said. "I'm looking for my son."

"Jackson?"

"That's right. Jackson Young. I heard about Michelle on the news. They said my boy is missing."

He seemed genuinely upset. He'd come out in the

storm with no jacket, unshaven. His dirty-blond hair was a riot on his head. Even his shoes were unmatched. Either he was a good actor or he wasn't involved with what happened to his wife and son.

"He is," Sharyn admitted. "We're looking for him now. Any idea where your wife was going?"

"Ex-wife," he corrected. "Michelle and I were divorced last year. She kept the house for her and Danny. I moved into Diamond Springs. I have no idea where she was going."

"She was dressed up; heels, no coat. We understand she's a nurse?"

"That's right. She wasn't going to work like that. What happened to her, Sheriff? They said on TV she was hit by a car."

"We don't know exactly what happened yet. We're trying to concentrate on finding your boy first. We were here too late to save your ex-wife."

He started crying, wiping the tears from his face as they fell. "I don't know what happened between us. She was seeing somebody. I don't know who. She said he was better than me. Said he knew more. I loved her. I just wasn't good enough for her."

"Let's not worry about that right now. We have to find Danny before it gets dark. We have to focus."

"What can I do?"

Not totally convinced he wasn't involved, she partnered him with Ernie to keep an eye on him. She didn't want him disappearing into the woods until after Daniel was found.

A steady stream of cars poured into Frog Meadow as evening settled in and the shadows of the snowy mountain tops became ghosts. The county rescue helicopter was able to get in on the search, large spotlights illuminating the snowy roads and forest paths where hundreds of flashlights bobbed in the darkness. Power had gone out earlier in the day and had still not been restored to the tiny crossroads community.

"What can we do to help, Sheriff?" Jolie and Harris Liston asked, bundled up with flashlights in hand.

Sharyn recognized the older couple from a murder investigation she'd conducted a few years back. Their only daughter had been killed in a local campground while Sharyn's grandfather was still sheriff forty years before. She had been looking for answers about another killing that seemed to copycat their daughter's death. "Thanks for coming out." She shook their hands. "Ernie can give you an area to search. But please don't wear yourselves out."

"We just want to help," Jolie said. "Nobody should have to lose their child. Bad enough the boy lost his mama."

"I appreciate your help. Did you know the Youngs?"

"Sure did. They seemed like a nice couple. Always

came to church." Harris nodded. "I'm a deacon, you know."

"Then it was like they fell apart," Jolie continued, her face half hidden in a gray wool scarf. "That young woman fell for a silver-tongued devil."

"Do you know who he is?"

They both shook their heads. Jolie answered, "We don't know him, Sheriff. He doesn't live around here. Drives a big, shiny car. One of those big square things the movie stars drive. Never saw the boy with them."

"You mean a Humvee?"

"Yeah," Harris agreed. "One of those military cars."

Sharyn thanked them again for coming out then took them to talk to Ernie. She rubbed her cold hands together and walked around the house again. Michelle was dressed up to go out with her lover. She wouldn't take Daniel with her. Daycare centers around the county were closed because of the weather. She had to take him to a relative or friend. She might have dropped him off and come back before she walked out to her death. The boy could be safe somewhere.

Her cell phone rang. "I've got some info for you," Trudy said. "Michelle's sister called in. Said she's been trying to call her sister for hours. Michelle was supposed to bring the little boy over there. She never showed up."

"Thanks, Trudy. Where is she?"

"On her way out there to help find the boy."

"Talk to you later." Sharyn saw Ernie running toward her, his breath coming cold and fast in the bright search lights from the helicopter. "What's up?"

"We found a gas can." He held up the red plastic container. "Neighbor said she was always running out of gas."

"She might have been on her way over there to get some when she was killed."

"The can was probably knocked out of her hand from the force of the hit. We couldn't see it right away because of the snow."

"Which puts the boy waiting for her in the car while she went to get enough gas to take him to her sister's house." Sharyn stared at the side of the house covered by the blowing snow. Some of it had melted when the sun came out, leaving a glistening crust, but between the cold air and night temperatures coming in, the majority of the snow was still there.

Ernie understood what she was saying as she said it. He grabbed a shovel from the back of his pickup and started digging through the heavy snow. Sharyn picked up the shovel Jeet Marts had left leaning against the side of the porch and dug alongside him until they heard a shovel blade hit metal.

By that time, hundreds of searchers were gathered around them. Word spread fast that they might have found the boy. Daniel's father dug with his bare hands, screaming his son's name, while the group brought every flashlight they could find to shine on the scene. The helicopter hovered above, spotlighting their work.

As soon as they realized the boy might be inside, the searchers dug at the snow that was left, clearing it with everything from their hands to cups and pieces of wood. A huge cheer went up when one of the flashlight beams caught on a patch of blue in the backseat and everyone recognized the small form of a child. One of the neighbors hefted an ax toward one of the windows.

"No!" Sharyn stopped him. "You could hurt him and damage evidence we may need to catch whoever killed his mother."

"Get one door clear." Ernie followed up on her instructions. "We can get him out from there."

Sharyn used her radio to call for the ambulance and paramedics who'd been waiting out on the road until they located the boy. She told the helicopter pilot to find someplace to land. "We can use your help to get the child to the hospital faster than the ambulance can get out on these roads."

"I'll set down on the road a'piece from you, Sheriff. Have the paramedics run the boy back to me and I'll keep the engine running."

Ernie got the door open and reached for the child who was still strapped in, but his father pushed his way past him and pulled the boy from the car seat. "Danny! Danny! Are you okay? Talk to Daddy. Tell Daddy you're all right."

The boy didn't open his eyes. His little face was pinched and blue with cold. His hands were in frozen claws from where he'd held them on the sides of the car seat, waiting for his mother who was never coming back for him.

The paramedics rushed in with blankets, but the father refused to relinquish his son to them.

"Let him go, Mr. Young. He needs their help." Ernie tried to convince him.

"No! I won't let him go again!"

"You'll kill him!" Harris Liston yelled. "Let him go!"

Sharyn put her arms around the little boy's cold body, refusing to release him when his father tugged to get him away. Her face was level with his above the boy's head. "Let him go. He'll die without help. You don't want that, do you?"

"No." Jackson Young sobbed. "I don't want to lose him again."

"Then let me have him. I'll make sure you see him right away." She tugged at the small body. "Let us help him."

Young held tight for another precious second then relented, giving Daniel to Sharyn. She rushed him back to the paramedics who wrapped him in blankets and ran back to the helicopter with him.

"Did he have a pulse?" Ernie asked when she came back.

"Faint. But it was there."

He sagged forward, wiping the fog from his glasses. "Thank God."

They stood close together with all the other searchers and watched the helicopter fly back up into the night sky. People prayed and waved. There was nothing more they could do. It was time to go home to their houses and hope the power was restored before too long.

"Anyone from Frog Meadow who wants to take shelter at the hospital for the night is welcome to ride back with us," Sharyn addressed the crowd. The fire chief added his own offer of transport as well.

No one took them up on their offer. Sharyn wasn't surprised. People who lived out in the county were an independent, stubborn lot. "All right. I want to say thanks to each of you for coming out. I'm sorry there isn't a reward for what you did here tonight. But when you see little Daniel again, you'll know he's alive because you were here."

The group murmured their acknowledgement of her words as they drifted off into the darkness, snow crunching under their feet. The cars started back to Diamond Springs and other towns.

The fire chief shook Sharyn's hand before he climbed back into his truck. "Good night's work, Sheriff. Let's hope none of these fine people fires up a kerosene heater before the night is over. I don't want to see you again tonight."

Sharyn agreed with him and wished him a good night before she turned to Ernie.

"Let's take Mr. Young with us. I have a few more questions to ask him." She watched the man being comforted by his former neighbors.

A young woman, who identified herself as Michelle's sister, met them as they walked back to the truck with her ex-brother-in-law. "Are you leaving? What about Danny? Did you find him?"

"We found him a few minutes ago." Sharyn nodded toward the ambulance headed toward Diamond Springs. "He's alive. They'll probably know more when they've had a chance to examine him."

"Are you arresting Jackson?" Her voice held as much concern for the father as it did for the nephew as her eyes flashed to his face.

"No. I'd like to ask him a few questions." Sharyn didn't miss the intimate glance. "You too, if you wouldn't mind coming down to the office."

"All right." She looked at Sharyn. "I don't know what else I can tell you."

"You might be surprised," Ernie said. "What's your name?"

"Brenda Farmer. Am I being arrested?"

"Is there some reason we *should* arrest you?" Sharyn asked her.

"No! I haven't done anything wrong. Jackson and I

have been good friends for years. But there's nothing wrong with that, right?"

Ernie smirked at Sharyn in the dim light from the truck cab. "If you'll just follow us to the office, Ms. Farmer. I'm sure you'll want to tell us whatever you can to catch the person who murdered your sister."

"Murdered her?" Brenda glanced at Jackson. "I thought it was a hit and run?"

"We think it might be a tad bit more than that," Ernie said. "If you'll follow us, we'll have some coffee and talk about it."

"Maybe I should talk to my husband first. Or call my lawyer."

Sharyn pushed her hat back on her head then stepped toward the other woman. "We can do this the nice way and you can follow us to the office, Ms. Farmer. Or we can put handcuffs on you and take you down in the back of the truck. Your choice."

Michelle's sister looked at Jackson who shrugged and climbed up into the back seat of the truck. "A-all right, Sheriff. I'll follow you down."

Sharyn didn't like the way that sounded. "Give me your driver's license."

"Why? Are you taking away my license because my sister was killed?"

"No. I want to make sure you're motivated to follow us."

"I *told* you I would."

Sharyn put out her hand. Brenda found her wallet and pulled out her driver's license, her fingers trembling so much she could hardly manage to move them. She gave it to Sharyn along with a look of angry defiance. "There!"

"We'll meet you at the office." Sharyn pocketed the license.

Sharyn and Ernie drove back to the station in the dark, mindful of the man in the back seat. But Sharyn knew Ernie was thinking the same thing she was. There was something going on between Jackson and Michelle's sister. Was that what broke up the marriage?

It hardly seemed like a good reason to kill Michelle. She and her husband were already apart. The chances seemed good neither of them were involved in the hit and run. But they might have other information that would help. Sharyn definitely wanted to know who Michelle's lover was. It was a good bet one or both of them knew.

Power was on in most of Diamond Springs by the time they got back to the office. Lights sprinkled across the sloping city leading down to the sheen of ice on Diamond Lake in the center of town.

Most of the county outside the city was without power. It would probably be days before their normal lives resumed. Wells with pumps would freeze and water pipes would crack. The chances were that someone would be poisoned with carbon monoxide trying to keep warm with their furnace off.

Sharyn had never thought of how repetitive it was sometimes. At least once a year, they had a major snow or ice storm and the results were predictable. It all seemed to rotate in the same patterns. Nothing ever changed.

"You okay?" Ernie asked when she was quiet for so long.

"I'm fine. Just tired. And I need a vacation. A *real* vacation. Not just a few days that I don't go into the office."

"You can go away, you know. We can handle it without you for a week."

She shook her head. "Not with Joe gone. Maybe when he comes back I'll get some skimpy outfits and get on one of those cruise ships that go to places with exotic names and have pink drinks with flowers and umbrellas in them."

Ernie chuckled as he pulled into the parking lot they shared with the courthouse. "Sounds like you have it down. Go for it, girl!"

Brenda Farmer pulled in right beside them. She slammed her door closed as she got out and marched up to Sharyn. "I talked to my husband on the way over here. He says you can't keep me here if I want to leave."

"That's true." Sharyn helped Jackson out of the truck. "But I know you both want to tell us all you can. Your sister was killed today, Ms. Farmer. And your nephew was almost taken as well. I know you both want to cooperate as much as possible so we can get the person responsible for this."

Brenda folded her arms across her chest and took a deep breath before she stalked into the basement office.

Jackson nodded to Sharyn. "I want to help in any way I can. I still loved Michelle, no matter what happened between us. I want to see whoever did this put away for a long time."

Sharyn and Ernie followed Jackson into the office. "Nice talkin'," Ernie remarked in an undertone.

"I expect some from you once we get them inside."

"You want me to take the girl?"

"That works for me."

Terry was back, filling out paperwork at his makeshift desk. He nodded to Sharyn and Ernie when he saw they had 'guests.' Ed was still out on the road, trying to resolve the ambulance situation. JP and Marvella were on their way back into the office.

They had to make do with the space they had in the basement. There was an old boiler room they'd turned into a conference/interrogation room. For the times they needed a second interrogation room, thankfully not often, they'd remodeled a supply closet. One questioner could get in there with one suspect.

Ernie took the smaller room without asking. Sharyn showed Jackson into the old boiler room. It was big enough to get in a folding table and four chairs.

"What can you tell me about Michelle's love interest?" she asked him as they sat down together.

"If she's seeing the same dude, the only thing I know about him is that he has money and lives on a big piece of land near Diamond Mountain. He's not from here. Came down from New York or Chicago."

Sharyn wrote down what he said. "Have you seen him?"

"Yeah." He shifted in his chair. "He's tall. Skinny. I don't know."

"Dark hair? Dark eyes?"

"Maybe." He glared at her. "Look, I answered your questions. I want to go and see my son."

"Just one more question." She paused as she wrote down what he said. "How long have you been sleeping with Brenda? Was that what broke up your marriage?"

He started to deny it. She could see it in his eyes. Then he hung his head and ran a hand around the back of his neck. "I don't know how it started."

"How long?"

"Michelle found out we were seeing each other and kicked me out. But she picked up with that other dude pretty fast. I think they knew each other before we broke up."

"But you don't know for sure?"

"No."

"Do you know what kind of car he drives?"

"A black Hummer, I think. There were some fancy wheels on it last time I saw it." He looked up at her with agony in his brown eyes. "Can I go now?"

"Yes." Sharyn got to her feet, noticing as she did that her pant legs and feet were cold and wet from trudging around in the snow. "I know you aren't leaving the county."

"No, ma'am."

"Thanks for coming in." Sharyn saw Brenda walk out of the closet door just a moment before she walked out of the conference room with Jackson. Marvella and JP came in as they left.

"What was that all about?" Marvella watched the couple leave.

"The sister and ex of our hit-and-run victim." Ernie sat down at his desk beside Sharyn's. "Not much help."

"He didn't know the lover's name. Did she?" Sharyn looked at her notes.

"Yep. Alan Michaelson."

"The ex-ADA?"

He shrugged. "That's what she said."

"And he drives a Hummer." Sharyn got to her feet, thinking about the last time she saw Michaelson. He was representing ex-senator Caison Talbot who was now set to be her new stepfather. Things had a way of going around in circles. "I think we might have to go and talk with Mr. Michaelson."

Ernie's face showed his disbelief. "Maybe we could wait until the morning to see him. It's nine-thirty. We've been here since six this morning. I'm beat."

"I'll go with you," Terry offered. "I've only been in since this afternoon."

Ernie glared at him. "I think the morning shift should go home and the night shift should stay."

"Where's Cari?" Sharyn wondered about her other night shift deputy.

"Having coffee with Toby." Terry shrugged. "As soon as we got back, he called to be sure she was okay."

"They're so *sweet!*" Marvella sighed. "I just love it!"

Sharyn got up and put on her jacket. "All of you go home. Terry, you can come with me to pay Michaelson a visit."

Ernie put his hand on her arm. "Could I have a word, Sheriff?"

They walked into the small conference room and closed the door while the deputies waited and strained to hear what they were saying.

"Sharyn, you can't go on like this. You can't stay here twenty-four hours a day. You have to go home and get some rest or you'll end up hurting yourself or someone else."

"I'm a big girl, Ernie. I know what I'm doing."

"I know you have a lot going on right now," he continued like he hadn't heard her. "But this isn't the way to get through it. Your daddy wouldn't have let a deputy stay on shift after shift this way."

"Good thing I'm the sheriff."

He stopped and stared at her. "Have you heard anything I've said to you?"

"I'm okay, Ernie. Don't worry."

"Go home, Sharyn. Take the night off and start over tomorrow. It will all be here when you get back."

"I can't." She smiled at him and patted his arm. "I'll see you in the morning."

He watched her walk out of the conference room then saw her put on her jacket and leave the office with Terry. Marvella and JP shook their heads. Whatever was wrong with the sheriff wouldn't be put right by a conversation in the conference room.

"Did you tell her she should go home?" Marvella demanded when he joined them.

"I said what I thought I should say." Ernie nodded at the closed basement door. "She's mule stubborn. She's gonna do what she thinks she has to do."

"Good thing for all of us." Marvella put her hands on her hips and her black curls bounced. "Otherwise I wouldn't be here."

Ernie sniffed. "Yeah, that would be a darn shame."

"Excuse me?" Marvella raised coal-black brows above whiskey-colored eyes. "Are you saying I'm not as good a deputy as anyone else here?"

"I'm saying I'm tired even if the sheriff isn't and I'm goin' home." Ernie put on his hat and coat. "You all should do the same. Even if the weather is better, there's gonna be all those people without power looking for someone to take it out on."

JP grinned when Marvella looked at him. "You are certainly a very good deputy."

She nodded. "That's right, partner. You're a good officer too."

Ernie rolled his eyes and walked out of the building into the cold before the mutual admiration society got the better of him. But bone weary as he was, he didn't go straight home to Annie. Instead he went to the basement morgue at the Diamond Springs Hospital where he knew he'd find Nick.

The medical examiner was sitting behind his heaped up desk drinking coffee that smelled as if it might be laced with something more than cream. If it was possible, his office was even more of a wreck than usual, but Ernie knew Nick could lay his hands on a file from last year without blinking twice.

Ernie closed the door behind him, shutting off the lab and the morgue itself from Nick's office. He was sure Keith and Megan were long gone for the night, but he wanted to be sure their conversation stayed private.

Nick looked up. "Slumming?"

"You know I never interfere," Ernie began, taking a seat in front of the desk.

"But you're about to make an exception?"

"I want to know what happened between you and Sharyn."

Nick's swarthy complexion blanched. "Go away."

"This is important." Ernie swore. "I need to know what I can do to help her."

"Leave it alone." Nick got to his feet and put on his heavy, black-rimmed glasses. "You can't help either of us."

Ernie stood up too and put his hand on Nick's arm. "I mean to try."

Chapter Four

"You know, I don't see what Cari sees in Toby Fisher, ADA," Terry told Sharyn as they drove to Alan Michaelson's home.

Michaelson started out as an assistant district attorney for Jack Winter, who was now state senator. He'd been an ADA to remember for Sharyn. He'd been there when she was first getting started as sheriff, taking particular pride in making her look stupid whenever possible. He'd finally challenged Jack, believing he could take him on.

After that mistake, he went on to work for Eldeon Percy, the present DA who was once one of the most notorious defense attorneys in the county. She couldn't help but wonder what Michaelson was up to now. Obviously doing better than he should as a junior partner at a law firm.

"You're a woman, Sheriff," Terry continued his rant. "Do you understand what she sees in him?"

"Michaelson?" Sharyn made the turn into one of the few driveways that was free of snow.

"*No!* Toby Fisher!"

Sharyn glanced at him in the dim light from the dash. "Are you infatuated with Deputy Long?"

"No." He coughed and sat up a little straighter. "What makes you say that?"

"You keep talking about her. When you're with her, you don't look at anyone else."

"Is it that obvious?"

"I hope she isn't worth your job."

Terry was barely twenty-three. He was a little naïve, but easy to joke with. He was a tall, muscular man who kept his head shaved and seemed tough, but Sharyn knew he had a strong sense of humor and was easygoing. He started out working for the Diamond Springs Police Department and later decided to join the sheriff's department after she saved his life. *Me and Nick.*

"Come on, Sheriff." Terry laughed. "Can't a man daydream on the job?"

"If it doesn't interfere." She pulled the truck into Michaelson's driveway. She could certainly testify to the problems with on-the-job relationships.

"I never let anything interfere with the job," he told her soberly. "Are we driving through that gate? It doesn't look like it's going to open."

Sharyn looked at the impressive ten-foot wrought iron gate mounted between two brick pillars. There was a call box on one of them that probably didn't work well without electricity. She allowed her gaze to drift toward the dark driveway beyond the gate and searched for any sign of light on the other side. If there was a house down there, it was impossible to tell.

"I think you're right." She shook the gate with her gloved hand. "I don't think we're going to get in this way."

Terry sized it up. "I have a friend who has a bulldozer. I could call him. He could be here in a few minutes."

She laughed. "You *are* dedicated, aren't you? I don't think we have to go to those extremes."

"How else are we going to get in? I don't think Michaelson is going to come down and open the gate for us."

Sharyn switched on her flashlight. The bright beam streamed through the darkness. She focused on the sides of the gate then moved to the far side of the brick pillars. "Most of the time these things are just for show. Somebody who really wants to get in will find a way." She put one leg through a gap between the gate pillar and the wrought iron fence connected to it. "I think I can squeeze through here. What about you?"

It was a tight squeeze, but she pushed through and waited on the other side for her deputy. Now all she had to worry about was Michaelson shooting them as intruders. That was saying they could find the house in the pitch black.

She waited a moment then called to Terry to see if he was able to squeeze through the gap. He answered standing beside her, making her jump. She couldn't see his smile, but she could hear it in his voice when he said, "I wanted to be sure we were prepared."

Sharyn shined her flashlight on him and saw the rifles he carried. He handed one to her with his big puppy grin. "I think we're prepared. Are you expecting to meet an army up there?"

"Always be prepared. That's my motto."

Together they walked up the tree-lined driveway keeping to the paved center. The snow on the ground and in the trees baffled the usual sounds of the forest. No bird calls broke the night, not even the sound of another vehicle on the road that went past the house.

"Spooky, huh?" Terry asked.

"Shh!" She stopped and pointed her rifle in the general direction of the woods to the right of them.

He crouched down and held his rifle at attention the same way. "What do you see?"

"Nothing," she returned. "Gotcha."

Sharyn smiled as she started walking again and Terry hustled to catch up. He was easy to be with. Not always looking out for her welfare like Ernie. Not difficult like Nick. *Nothing like Nick.*

The drive opened with the trees parting on each side. A huge house, the multi-leveled roof blanketed with snow, stood before them like a fairy tale castle from a storybook.

"Wow!" Terry appreciated the size and expense of the house. "What did you say this guy does for a living?"

"I didn't. When I knew him, he was assistant district attorney. Makes you wish you'd gone to law school, huh?"

"No way. I couldn't sit still that long. I heard you were almost one of *them.* What happened?"

"It's a long story. I think we should knock on the door and hear Mr. Michaelson's story instead."

Terry nodded and preceded her to the wide front door. He raised and lowered the heavy knocker. The sound echoed around them. He sniffed the crisp air. "Do you smell something?"

"Smells like car exhaust. I don't hear a car."

"It could be coming from the house. When I was a paramedic, we went out on a case where this guy left the car running in the garage while his wife and daughters got ready for church. It was cold and they didn't want to get in a cold car. He asphyxiated himself and his family."

"Nice story." She looked at the big door in front of them. "Is it locked?"

He tried it. "No." He put his nose to the doorframe. "The smell is definitely coming from inside the house."

"I'd say we don't have time for a search warrant." Sharyn opened the door and an alarm screamed out at them. "I guess the power is on after all."

"We can't go in there, Sheriff. We don't know where it's coming from. We could end up dead like that family I was telling you about."

"You're right. Stay here. Call for backup and see if you can get any kind of medical unit out here."

He watched as she covered her face with her scarf and disappeared into the house. He called for backup and paramedics, then swore as he followed her into the house.

Michaelson's home was built like a monstrous Swiss chalet. It was four levels with carved banisters and large windows. Sharyn switched on the lights as she went, carefully making her way through the rooms and down toward the ground floor. The back of the house went lower than the front. All the walls that faced the mountain were made of glass.

She stared at one of them, realizing Terry was right. She could feel the effects of the carbon monoxide. She wouldn't make it down to the lowest level where she suspected the garage might be. She heard Terry come up behind her and realized he hadn't followed orders to wait for her.

Without another thought, she picked up a heavy chair and sent it crashing through one of the windows.

Terry came and stood beside her as they both gulped in huge breaths of clean air. "You know this would be bad if the house was on fire."

"I know. Good thing it's not."

When they could breathe again and shook off the dizziness, they moved toward the ground floor again. Sharyn went first and Terry checked behind them. They called for Michaelson but there was no answer. Sharyn had a feeling he might never answer a summons again if he was here in this house.

The ground floor was actually dug into the side of the mountain. It contained a long game room with a pool table and video games. The double doors at the far end were open to the garage. Sharyn looked at Terry, again beginning to feel the effects of the carbon monoxide poisoning, and shook her head. He agreed wordlessly and they proceeded through the doors.

Sharyn found the button to open the four outside doors on the garage. Terry switched on the lights. In the first bay, there was a full-sized, black Humvee that was running. The other three bays included a classic Corvette, a Jeep and a Lamborghini.

Terry whistled. "Nineteen-sixty-six Corvette Maco Shark convertible. Sweet."

"Let's see if Michaelson is down here." Sharyn moved to the driver's side of the Humvee and tried to open the door. "It's locked." She cupped her hands on the tinted window to try and see inside. "It's too dark."

"Allow me." Terry picked up a heavy wrench and broke the window. He reached his hand inside and pulled up the lock. Alan Michaelson fell sideways from the driver's seat.

Sharyn caught him as the security company that monitored his alarm system pulled inside the garage. Four men jumped out of the vehicle and drew their weapons, yelling, "Freeze! Put your hands in the air where we can see them."

Terry immediately aimed his rifle at them. "I don't think so. You put *your* guns down."

Sharyn checked Michaelson's pulse before looking up at the standoff situation. "All right. Let's all put the guns down. I'm the sheriff and this is my deputy. We'll handle the problem. Thank you for coming."

The four men looked reluctant to comply, possibly uncertain about their position in such an event. Terry didn't move or alter the way he held his rifle.

Sharyn sighed and said, "Terry, put the rifle down and help me with Michaelson." She looked up at the other men. "You can come and take a look at my badge if you like, but I wouldn't advise it. Those sirens you hear are our backup. You did a fine job, but you need to stand down so the paramedics can get in here and get this man to the hospital."

The lead security guard nodded and gestured to the

other men to get back in the vehicle. "We'll wait out here. We have to fill out a D-four-one-one-seven form on this and we'll need someone's signature."

Sharyn didn't respond as she and Terry slowly lowered Michaelson to the garage floor. Terry shook his head. "It won't do much good to take him to the hospital."

"I know." She looked at the Humvee. There was some damage to the left front panel. "I think we found our hit-and-run driver. Or at least the vehicle."

"So he kills his lover then comes home to his estate and kills himself. That sounds pretty stupid. Especially with a Maco Shark in his garage. What kind of man owns a car like that and kills himself?"

"A man who feels remorse for killing someone," she supposed. "Maybe even the Maco Shark couldn't make up for that."

"Maybe." His tone doubted that wisdom.

The paramedics were there followed closely by JP and Marvella. While Terry called the ME's office, Sharyn had her other two deputies make sure the crime scene was preserved from further disruption. She looked over the Humvee and the area in the garage around it.

The Humvee doors were locked. And why bother leaving the doors to the house open when he was sitting in the vehicle? When Terry got off the phone with Nick, she had him thoroughly check out the rest of the house in case Michaelson was taking someone else with him.

But the house was empty. It could've been that Michaelson didn't care or notice that the doors to the house were open. Even the locked Humvee doors could be explained by accidentally locking them with the remote when he started the vehicle.

"I don't see anything unusual out here or in the house," Terry said. "I think if we find out this Hummer matches up with our hit and run, we can mark it down as a murder/suicide. Maybe his lady friend wanted somebody else."

"We don't see much of that around here," Marvella said. "But this doesn't look like a murder scene to me, so that must be what happened."

Nick was arriving as Sharyn cautioned all of them against speculation. "We don't know what happened here until all of the facts are in."

Only Keith was with Nick this time. Sharyn swallowed hard and hoped her resolve would hold up talking to Nick face to face. She took him aside as his assistant began processing the scene. "This *looks* like a suicide."

Nick nodded. "But something about it bothers you?"

"Yeah. I don't know what exactly." She told him about the locked doors and the house being left open to the garage. "It might not be anything, but . . ."

"I'll check it out. I assume you're thinking this could be the hit-and-run vehicle?"

"Right. That's why we were here. Michaelson was dating the victim from Frog Meadow."

"*Alan* Michaelson?" Nick looked around. "Who died and made him king?"

"I don't know. But I'm going to find out."

"I'll let you know when I have something from my end."

Her eyes met his. "Thanks."

He didn't reply. There was so much more to say between them that couldn't be said, at least not in Michaelson's garage surrounded by emergency workers. It might never be said.

Despite Terry's thorough search of the premises, Sharyn went through the house again looking for a suicide note or anything else that could speak to Michaelson's frame of mind before his death. She was interested in who he was working for as well. But the thousand-dollar suits in his closets and the expensive hand-woven rugs on his floors didn't tell her what she needed to know.

Terry, Marvella and JP found her in Michaelson's office, the large windows seeing sunrise peeking over Diamond Mountain. The pale pink and orange rays illuminated the whitened landscape, throwing the craggy face of the mountain in sharp relief.

"We've bagged, measured, and processed everything

we could," Terry told her. "It's almost seven. Nick and Keith left a little while ago. Do you want me to bring the truck up and get you?"

Sharyn looked up at him, focusing her eyes away from the documents she'd been reading. "Have you figured out if anything was wrong with the call box at the gate last night?"

The three deputies looked at one another. Marvella shrugged. "I didn't know there *was* anything wrong with it."

"When we came up last night it wasn't working," Sharyn said. "We thought the power was off. I need someone to check it and find out if anything is wrong with it."

Terry glanced at his watch. "I thought we could leave a note about that for Ernie. He and Ed should be in the office by now."

"They'll have a pile of accidents, road closings, and power outages to deal with," Sharyn replied, looking back at the papers in her hand. "Marvella, you and JP go home and get some sleep. Terry, find out why the call box didn't work. Call an electrician or whoever you have to until we have an answer."

"You got it, Sheriff." Terry stared at her a minute longer as Marvella and JP turned to leave. "What about you? I can run you back to the office and I'll come back out and check the call box."

"That's okay. I'll be here while you check it."

Terry ran his hand around the back of his neck. "Sheriff, you've been working since yesterday morning about this time. I know it's not my place to speak out, but . . ."

"You're right. It's not your place. Let me know when you've figured out what happened to the call box."

"Yes, ma'am."

He closed the door to the office quietly behind him as he left. Sharyn sat back in the expensive, leather chair and closed her eyes, willing her brain to keep functioning. She wasn't ready to go home yet. There were two deaths waiting to be explained and a host of weather-related emergencies to be handled.

She stood up and looked out of the ten-foot window, staring at the blue sky for a long time. She realized she wouldn't be able to solve anything if she fell apart now. She had to keep going. The answers were close at hand. Sometimes she felt like she could reach out and touch them. Sometimes they felt as far away as the moon.

There was a small bathroom beside Michaelson's office. She went there and splashed some water in her face, noting that she looked like one of the undead in a bad horror movie. Her bright red hair made it seem all that much more realistic. Didn't vampires have red hair?

Starving, she went down to the kitchen and found a banana. She wasn't sure if she was supposed to eat it or not, but technically it wasn't part of the crime scene and it was too ripe to last another day. She wished she had a large mocha latte, but that wasn't going to happen. She was going to have to do with the banana and a glass of water.

Ernie called her cell phone to ask if there was any progress. Sharyn swallowed the last of the banana and told him what she knew so far. It wasn't much. Even worse, she was almost too tired to care if Michaelson died a suicide or a homicide.

"I got an email from Joe today," Ernie said. "He's coming home. He could be here as early as Friday."

She felt better. "That's great! Have you talked to Sarah yet?"

"Yep. She got the same email. I think we should try to set up a little welcome home party as soon as we have confirmation on the day and time. It will be good to see Joe back home where he belongs."

"Yeah. We could sure use his help. How are things at the office?"

"You know. It's always the same after a storm." He paused for a moment. "Don't make me come up there and get you. Your shift is over. Go home."

"In point of fact, my shift just began. But I'll be back as soon as Terry has some word on the call box." She explained what happened when they tried to get in the gate.

"So you're looking for something more than a suicide?"

"I'm not sure." She looked around herself at the expensive, plush surroundings. "Something doesn't feel right."

"Another Sheriff Sharyn Howard gut instinct?"

"Maybe. Or maybe not. We'll see. Keep me posted."

"I won't. And don't bother coming back to the office. Have Terry take you home. If you show your face here before tomorrow, I'll run you off with a switch."

Sharyn laughed and closed her cell phone. She went back to Michaelson's office, going through his desk and file cabinet. Whatever he did for a living, he kept it pretty well hidden. There were no check stubs, no records of any transactions. She looked at the laptop on his desk. It was probably all in there, but when she tried to access it, it refused to oblige her, demanding a password.

She called Ernie back and asked him if Cari was still there. "I'm bringing Michaelson's computer back for her to take apart. I can't find anything here, including a suicide note. Maybe he left it all on the computer."

Ernie told her Cari was working over and would be there to take a look at it. Sharyn thanked him and started to call Terry to see if there was any progress on the call box. Instead, she got out of the house that still reeked of carbon monoxide to find out for herself.

The cold air felt good against her face. She filled her lungs with it, buried her hands in her pockets and walked quickly down the drive. Already, the trees were shaking off the fluffy snow as the sun warmed the day. Snow never lasted in Montgomery County. It came and was gone, thank goodness. There weren't enough deputies to make it through a northern-type winter.

The driveway didn't seem so long with the daylight and the sunshine. She looked back at Michaelson's house, still amazed that a man who was an ADA only a few years ago could afford it. She didn't remember hearing that he had inherited a fortune from some relative. It seemed to her that she might have even heard about him building what amounted to a mansion for Diamond Springs.

Was his newfound wealth involved in his death? She hoped Nick might have some answers for her when she got back to town.

Terry was still looking at the call box as she walked through the open wrought iron gate. He saw her and waved. "I was about to call you."

"I thought I'd save you all that button-pushing. What's up?"

"Nothing. All the wires are connected. I checked inside before I came down. Everything looked okay in there. I had JP call me from the box as he went out. It works now. Maybe the power was off when we first came up. Maybe it came back on while we were walking toward the house."

"Did you call an electrician?"

"Yep. But he probably won't be here anytime soon. With all the outages all over the county, he's busy. I could try someone else."

"That's okay. It's not going anywhere. We can get our answers tomorrow. For now, we'll have Ernie talk to the security people. They must have known the code to get in. The gate wasn't open when we were here."

"I hope all that ends with a 'let's go back to the office now.' "

She smiled. "I think we've done all we can do here. We have to go back up and get Michaelson's laptop for Cari to work on. After that, we'll leave."

"Great!"

Terry let Sharyn out at the door to go back in for the laptop. She went quickly up the stairs and returned to Michaelson's office. She unplugged the laptop from the wall and picked it up.

She trusted Terry but she knew someone was spying on the sheriff's department for what was left of the good-old-boys network that ran Diamond Springs behind the scenes.

That person was responsible for David Matthews' death as surely as if he or she pulled the trigger on the gun that killed him. It wasn't the same gun that killed her father, but she was betting the same people were behind it.

She'd thought she had them a few other times with her father's journal she'd managed to decode, and the men in state prison who were ready to tell her who paid them to kill him. Both of those chances were taken away from her. She didn't plan to lose this one.

She planned to ask DA Percy some questions about Michaelson. She knew he could be part of the group responsible for so much of the shadowy crime in the county. That group included many of Diamond Springs' elite citizens: a few judges, businessmen and now ex-senator Caison Talbot, who was too smart to talk about what he knew after almost losing everything, including his life.

Proving what she suspected was another matter, but she was determined to try. This investigation might have nothing to do with the people who killed her father and David, but she wasn't taking any chances with information until she knew the truth.

"I think I'll let you take me home before you go to the office," she told Terry when they got back to town.

"That's a good idea, Sheriff. I'll take this to Cari and let her see what she can figure out."

The streets of Diamond Springs were almost clear. The shiny wet blacktop glared through white streaks that were rapidly melting under the warm sun. There were piles of snow pushed up by the plow, but since the town had only one plow, only a few streets were affected.

Sharyn's apartment was only a few blocks from Diamond Lake in one direction and a few blocks from the office in the other. The plow didn't make it that far from

Main Street. Snow still covered the street and sidewalk, but even that was turning quickly to slush. She left the laptop on the truck seat between them and thanked Terry for the ride.

"Since Ernie didn't want me in the office today, tell him he can drive my Jeep over this evening. I'll see you tomorrow."

Terry told her to have a good night and left her at the curb. Sharyn watched him leave. Things had been quiet in Diamond Springs since David's death and the FBI's investigation following it. But as Agent Brewster had foretold, no arrests were made. Michaelson's death could mean another shakeup in the organization. She was taking a chance there would be information on the computer she needed.

Going up the narrow stairs to her apartment, her heart was pounding, all feelings of being tired gone in the surge of adrenaline from the night's activities. Her fingers trembled as she opened the door to her apartment.

"Hello, Sharyn." Jack Winter stepped out of the shadows in the hall. He put his hand on her shoulder and lowered his lips to hers. "I'm glad you were finally able to come home."

Chapter Five

"What a surprise!" Sharyn said with a smile, though the effort was almost too much for her. The touch of his hand, his lips on hers, were enough to make her scream. But she didn't. She didn't scream or run away as she'd wanted to for the past three months.

She'd devised the plan with Agent Brewster that day in the cemetery. They all knew who was responsible for David's death and so many other terrible things that happened in Diamond Springs. Sharyn believed Jack had her father killed as well. No matter what she had to do, she was going to prove it.

The plan was simple considering that Jack had always made his interest in her plain. Breaking up with

Nick had been the hardest part. She couldn't explain what she was going to do.

It wasn't that she didn't trust him to know the truth. She couldn't take a chance that they could be seen together outside of work. She wasn't afraid for herself, but she didn't want to take a chance with Nick's life or his career. Jack had broken other people, like Caison Talbot and Jill Madison-Farmer. He'd ruined their lives. She wouldn't let that happen to Nick.

Nick was suffering right now, as she was suffering. But she was the sheriff and she owed her father, David, and all the other people who'd been hurt by Jack and his good-old-boys network, a chance for justice. She was going through with the plan no matter that her heart was breaking and her skin crawled when Jack touched her.

"Come inside." She opened the door and stood to one side, likening herself to the spider and seeing Jack as the fly. "I hope you weren't waiting long."

"Not long. I knew you'd be coming home soon."

"Oh? Have you added being psychic to your accomplishments?" She took his coat and closed the door behind him.

"With you, dear." He lingered by the door to touch her face. "Long night?"

She told him about the hit and run in Frog Meadow and about Alan Michaelson's death. As she spoke, she started a pot of coffee. "It looks like Michaelson killed himself."

"He was a good man. Unfortunate circumstances."

Sharyn agreed with him, staring into his pale blue eyes and round-featured face. His thinning hair was the color of spring wheat, almost too fine to see. There was a keen sense of perception about him as though he heard more than what was said. She knew he was ambitious. Diamond Springs felt the difference when he took over as head of the network behind drugs and crime in town.

It was probably her imagination that made her think he could see through her. If he suspected anything, he didn't let on. She didn't believe he'd play this game with her if he didn't think he could win.

"There might be something more to it," she added to see his reaction. "It might not be suicide."

His brows lifted. "No? Were there questionable conditions?"

"A few. I'm looking into them." Pouring the coffee into two mugs, she turned back to him, but he'd gotten up from the chair in her living room and joined her.

"You've been sheriff a long time, Sharyn. I think you'd know a suicide when you see one."

"Maybe." She handed him his coffee. "But there are a few things that don't make sense."

"It sounds like Michaelson killed his girlfriend, for

whatever reason, then couldn't take it and killed himself. Case closed. I wouldn't have encouraged you to pursue this when I was district attorney. I'm not encouraging you to pursue it now."

He sounded like he was telling her not to ask any more questions. That perked her interest. Maybe she was right about Michaelson's death. This might be what she was looking for. "But I owe it to Michaelson to find out what happened."

Jack put his hand on her shoulder and looked into her face as though he could compel her to change her mind. "Sometimes things are better left alone."

Sharyn didn't respond, shifting her gaze from his. "You might be right." She changed the subject. "What brings you down from the Capitol?"

"You, of course. It's been a few days and I missed you. I thought maybe we could have dinner after I attend to some other business."

Was it possible Jack personally took care of whatever problem he was having with Michaelson? His presence here in the middle of the week while the legislature was in session was suspicious. It was hard to imagine Jack getting his hands dirty with Michaelson's death, but maybe there was no other way to do it.

"Sounds good. Let me catch a fast shower and change clothes. I'm not going into the office today. We could spend the whole day together."

"Much as I'd like that, I have to take care of a few

things. You understand. I'll come by when I'm finished and pick you up. I hope you aren't too disappointed."

"That's okay. I understand. You're an important man."

He put his arm around her. "You *are* disappointed. I'm sorry. Maybe this will help." He pulled out a jeweler's box and gave it to her. "I only wish it was as beautiful as you."

Sharyn smiled and happily opened the ornate red box to find an expensive diamond pendant inside. "It's exquisite! You shouldn't have!"

"Of course I should." He kissed her and took the delicate gold chain from her to clasp it around her throat. "I love the way it looks on you. You're a beautiful woman, Sharyn. I'm a lucky man to have you."

She looked at the two of them in the mirror near her door. She couldn't even try to pretend it was Nick there with her to get through it. She focused on her plan, on succeeding in bringing this man to his knees. She passionately wanted to see him in prison for his crimes. That was the emotion that would see her through. He'd make a mistake and when he did, she wanted to be there.

"I have to go now," he told her. "I'll see you about seven. Try to get some rest. And be sure to wear the pendant with your best dress tonight. We're going some place special."

She smiled and kissed him good-bye, closed the door when he was gone, and slid to the floor. She was too exhausted, too sick with the charade she was playing. She didn't know how much longer she could keep going. Her hand touched the pendant and almost ripped it off her neck.

Never the type of person to act like someone she wasn't, pretending to care about Jack, to bend to his considerable will, was at the limit of what she could do. She wanted to hike up into the mountains and never come back. She wanted to forget the last few months had happened. She wanted Nick back in her life.

But steely resolve drove her to her feet. She carefully put the diamond pendant on the dresser in her bedroom beside the other tokens Jack had given her. Then she ripped her uniform off and went to take a shower.

The phone rang as she was zipping up her jeans and pulling a sweater over her head. It took half an hour, all the hot water and a stern self talking to before she could face the world again. But now she was ready to take on what she knew was her responsibility.

She expected to hear Ernie or someone else from the office when she answered the phone. Instead, it was her Aunt Selma, wanting to know if they could have lunch. Sharyn had no definite plans until dinner so she was glad to spend time with her favorite aunt.

It was unusual for Selma to drive into Diamond Springs. She kept busy on the family farm outside of town, especially since she'd married Sam Two-Rivers in a quiet service a few months ago.

Sam hated town even worse than Selma, if that was possible. Sharyn supposed he might be out working with animal preservation after the storm. Maybe Selma was lonely without him. The two of them were inseparable since they'd met a few years back.

Sharyn agreed to meet Selma at a new Greek restaurant that opened near the old bridge on Diamond Lake. It was one of the few places she'd never been with Nick.

He was working, probably at the college, where he taught psychology and forensics, and trying to finish the autopsies on the two victims. He was always stretched during times when the county needed him to work as medical examiner. They couldn't pay him enough to give up his job teaching, not that she was sure he would.

She couldn't think about Nick. It was too painful. They might never be together again. She planned to tell him the truth once Jack was in prison, but she didn't know if he would forgive her. She would never forget the look on his face when she told him it was over between them. She wasn't sure she would ever forgive herself.

She wished there was someone she could tell, someone she could confide in without fear they would intervene. Her mother was out of the question. Faye Howard was thrilled that her daughter was dating a senator, even if it was a man *she'd* thought of dating a few years back. Sharyn considered telling Selma about it, but

Selma had history with Jack too. Jack seemed to have a thing for the Howard women.

There was no one who could tell her if what she was doing was right or wrong. She would have to keep her own counsel and hope she was strong enough to see this through. So many times when she wasn't sure what to do she could ask herself what her father or grandfather would do in a similar circumstance. But she was uniquely alone in this case. Neither Jacob nor T. Raymond would have found themselves pretending to be in love with a man to trap him in incriminating circumstances that could put him in prison for the rest of his life.

Sharyn got to the restaurant early, walking down the big hill that seemed to drop right into the lake. The sun had melted most of the snow though some still lingered in shaded areas. Folds of it refused to move from tarps covering boats moored at the marina. The old bridge that was begun but never finished dripped water even as transplanted seagulls called from the top of it.

She stepped inside the Athenos Restaurant and smiled at the painted images of the Acropolis and ancient temples. Grapes and grape leaves twined around artificial pillars that created interesting spots for secluded tables. There was a long bar with statues of Zeus, Poseidon, and Hermes presiding over wine glasses and drink menus. The whole effect was different than any other restaurant in town. She couldn't wait to try their food.

A nervous waiter greeted her. Sharyn had to look down to make sure she was wearing her jeans. People usually looked uneasy when she was in uniform. Her gun was concealed in her shoulder holster beneath her jacket. But she supposed most people in town knew who she was without the uniform. It wasn't a large enough place to get lost in the crowds.

To her surprise, Selma was already seated at a back table that overlooked the lake. She wasn't alone. The conversation between her, Sam, and Caison was so heated, Selma didn't even notice Sharyn's arrival.

Sharyn almost turned around and left. The only way this could be worse would be if her mother was present. It was bad enough to see Caison at a table with Selma who thoroughly disliked him. It didn't bode well for what they had to say if it was bad enough for them to team up.

Too late. Selma glanced up and saw her. She waved and smiled and Sharyn knew she was trapped. She could pretend there was an emergency of some kind, but otherwise she was going to have to listen to whatever the trio had to tell her.

Possibly sensing Sharyn's discomfort, Selma got to her feet and walked over to meet her niece. "It's been a while since I saw you last. I guess they're keeping you pretty busy."

"You know how that goes." Sharyn's eyes narrowed on the two men at the table who were looking at her. "Is it safe to have lunch or should I skip it for an emergency call?"

"I think you can handle it." Selma laced her arm through Sharyn's as though worried she might change her mind. They walked toward the table and the two men got to their feet.

"Nice to see you, Sharyn." Caison extended his hand toward her. "Sorry your mother couldn't be here." There was no casual explanation about why Faye was absent.

Sam nodded at Sharyn. "You haven't been out to the house lately. We've decided to keep some goats. Selma is interested in making goat milk cheese and soap."

Sharyn shook hands with both men then sat down beside her aunt. "Cheese, I've heard of. Soap out of goat's milk?"

Selma and Sam explained about their new project with their usual enthusiasm. Sharyn glanced up as the waiter brought them glasses of water. Caison looked impatient. Whatever brought him out with his unlikely companions was something he was ready to get over with.

The conversation about goats ran down quickly to awkward silence. The waiter kept looking at them, waiting for some signal they were ready to order. Selma picked up her menu and read through it. "You like spanakopita, don't you, Sharyn?"

"Oh for goodness sake," Caison finally burst out. "We came for a reason. We might as well talk about it. It won't get better pretending we're here to eat."

"I'm here to eat." Sharyn didn't look up from her menu. "I think I'll have some baklava too."

"We're here for a reason," Selma agreed. "But I think we could still eat lunch."

"It's ridiculous to pretend we don't have something important to say," Caison continued. "Who cares what's on the menu?"

Sam glared at him but didn't say anything, stubbornly looking at his menu. Selma, however, was never a woman who could be ignored. She pushed back the falling crown of white-red hair and put down her menu. "Caison, I wouldn't have agreed to let you come today if I'd known you were going to be rude. Settle down. This is a civilized conversation. We can at least order our meals before we talk."

Caison nodded and kept his mouth shut as he picked up his menu.

But the tone of the impending conversation was starting to sound like something Sharyn should avoid. "I think I'm already getting indigestion and I haven't eaten."

"Pick out what you want to eat for lunch so the nice waiter can quit hovering," Selma told her. "I happen to know you aren't working today, so sit back and enjoy your lunch."

The waiter came and smilingly took their orders. Sharyn wished she could talk him into staying, but he was gone as soon as he had the last of Sam's lunch order. Apparently the tone of the coming conversation scared him too.

Selma folded her hands on the table and looked at her niece who was more like her in appearance and demeanor than she was like Faye. There was more stalwart Howard blood in her. It made her strong and healthy, like her daddy and his daddy before him. But it also made her stubborn and argumentative. Once she was set on a course, it was almost impossible to get her to go another way. "You know I don't like to interfere."

"I know when you say that you're about to interfere a lot," Sharyn told her.

"Only for your own good." Selma's blue eyes focused on her.

"We only want to help," Sam agreed. "Just hear us out."

"Never mind all that whitewash." Caison fixed his still-impressive stare on Sharyn. "You're asking for trouble, young woman. And don't think it won't come knocking on your door when you least expect it."

Sharyn smiled a little. If she had any idea what they were talking about, she might be *really* scared. As it was, she was hoping the food would arrive while they all meandered around the subject. That way she could hide behind the pretext that she was eating. A person could hardly answer the charges brought against her with a mouthful of food.

"We're talking about Jack, of course," Selma said quietly. "I'd have no problem with you taking your grandfather's gun and shooting that snake. But you can't possibly think I believe you care for him. I shudder to think about you kissing him or spending time with him."

Sharyn didn't reply. She'd had plenty of warnings that this was coming. No one was happy about her dating Jack. But she didn't plan to let on that she felt the same way. She'd wished many times it was as easy as pulling out her gun and killing him, but she would never know the truth about what happened to David or her father if she did that.

"That man almost killed me." Caison's voice was like slipping silk over sandpaper. "He probably *would* have killed me, but he wanted to watch me squirm."

"If you hate him so much," Sharyn pinned him down, "why didn't you offer to testify against him? Why didn't you take care of the problem a long time ago?"

Caison sat back in his chair, his shock of white hair making his ruddy complexion seem darker. "You know I wouldn't last a day in this town if I did that. The Feds offered to relocate me, give me a new life and a new name. But my life and my name mean something to me."

Sharyn sipped some water. "I'm sorry you think all of this has happened to you because of Jack. But I'm sure since you're an officer of the court, you'd find some way to tell the truth if you really believed what you're saying."

Caison stared at her. "Your daddy was always too lenient with that mouth of yours. I wash my hands of it. I have enough to do trying to get my boy out of prison where *you* put him."

Selma intervened. "I hardly think now is the time to talk to Sharyn about your son who tried to kill both of you before she took him in."

Sharyn was thinking the same thing. She looked at Sam. "What's your take on all this?" She thought she might as well hear it all before she left.

Sam shrugged his broad shoulders. His black hair was beginning to show a few strands of white at the temples, but his face still looked exactly the same as the day she met him. "I only came out because Selma asked me to. I think you should do what you've always done since I've known you, Sharyn. What you think is right."

"Sam!" Selma complained. "*You* could've stayed home too."

"She asked for my opinion. I gave it."

Sharyn played with the piece of lemon in her water glass. Where was lunch? Could she leave without hearing anything else about Jack?

"I love you as if you were my own daughter," Selma

said. "You know that I know Jack too well. And I know *you* too. There has to be some motivation that drove you to break up with Nick and start dating Jack. I haven't said anything until now because I thought you'd come to your senses. I can't stay quiet anymore. You have to stop seeing him before you get hurt."

Sharyn didn't speak at first. How could she tell her aunt that it was Selma's own story about how Jack ruined the man she'd planned to marry that made Sharyn drive Nick away? She couldn't tell her the truth, especially in front of Caison. She didn't trust him completely. He might be willing to give her away if it meant getting back in Jack's good graces.

The food finally came and Sharyn busied herself eating. The other three stared at her then started eating too. She hoped that would be it on the subject.

"I wouldn't think you'd be so taken in by him," Caison said. "The man is almost old enough to be your grandfather. He's evil besides, and mark my words; he'll take something precious from you. You'd best get away from him while you can."

Sharyn smiled. "Thank you for your concern. But I've decided to take my mother's advice for once. She's not here because she likes Jack and she's glad I'm seeing him. I wish all of you could see him the way I do. He's a good man."

Selma made polite gagging noises into her napkin

and pushed the rest of her food away. "I don't think I can stomach anything else with that kind of talk. I hope you'll think about this. You've always been so clever. I can't believe you can't see the devil when he's standing right in front of you."

Caison abruptly put his napkin and a wad of money on the table. "I have things to do. If you need me, Sharyn, you know where to find me."

Selma and Sam got to their feet a few minutes later. Sam was still trying to finish his sandwich, but Selma was ready to go. "I'll try not to bring this up again with you, Sharyn," Selma promised. "You have the right to make the wrong decision. I just hope it doesn't cost you more than you realize."

Sam smiled and squeezed Sharyn's shoulder as Selma walked away from the table. "Take care."

Sharyn forced herself to sit at the table and drink more water and eat a little more of the delicious food. She didn't want to confront her three lunchmates in the parking lot. She'd never been very good at lying, but suddenly found herself living a lie. It was hard enough without having to face down Selma and Sam, two people she cared very much about.

Caison's opinion didn't mean much to her. He might plan to marry her mother, but he was tainted with the same sins that made Jack guilty.

Before she could get up to leave, ex-defense attorney Jill Madison-Farmer sat down beside her and started eating the food that was left over. She asked the waiter for more water and smiled at Sharyn. "How's it going? Sounds like you could use a friend."

Sharyn didn't count Jill as a friend exactly. Since Jill had lost her career trying to help her, she was more like a dependent. There were all sorts of rumors about her life. She mostly lived on the street, had lost custody of her children, and seemed to wander aimlessly trying to get revenge on Jack for what he did to her.

"Thanks," Sharyn said. "How are you doing?"

"Fine. Things are good considering I was branded a drug addict and lost everything because of your new love interest."

"You don't know for sure it was Jack that set you up. It could've been anyone."

Jill looked under the table then back up at Sharyn's face. "Just checking to see if his hand was up your back making the Sharyn puppet move and talk. Did you take a whack on the head or something? How can you sit there and spout that stuff at me? You know, we *both* know, what happened."

"I think you should get on with your life." Sharyn got to her feet and put her jacket back on.

"What life? He took everything from me. But I was thinking . . ." Jill got up and stood close to Sharyn, her tall, thin frame bordering on gaunt. Her brown hair looked uncombed. She had always been so meticulous in her appearance when she was the number one defense attorney to call in town. "You're very close to him. You could shoot him and I could help you drop his body in the lake."

"That sounds a little messy."

"Maybe. What about poison? That would be cleaner. If you don't like the lake idea, we could take him up in the mountains and let the bears eat him."

Sharyn turned suddenly when they walked outside. "I've told you this before. You have to put this behind you. Go on with your life. Whatever happened is over. Killing Jack or anyone else won't make it better."

Jill grinned, showing spaces where she was missing teeth. "I can't go on as long as he's alive. Think about it, Sharyn. Call me if you change your mind." She wiped her nose on her sleeve. "Can you lend me a twenty?"

Sharyn gave her thirty dollars, all she had in her wallet. "Buy yourself some clean clothes. I'll talk to you later."

Jill took the money and wandered off. Sharyn started back home. Talking to Jill was harder than pretending to Selma that she loved Jack. She knew Jill was right about him. She wished she *could* shoot him and dump him in the lake. It would be so much easier than trying to bring him to justice. Her conscience bothered her about Jill, but she was close to engineering Jack's downfall. She couldn't be distracted by her heart now.

She was almost home when her cell phone rang in her pocket. It was Ernie, and for a moment, she thought he was going to ask her to come in and help out. But he had different news. "Joe is on his way home! He and a few buddies from this area hitched a ride with someone. He'll be landing at the airport in half an hour. Sarah wasn't going to say anything because he asked her not to. He was afraid we'd make a big deal out of it. Can you imagine?"

Sharyn laughed. "Did you contact the Goodyear blimp in time or are we going to have to make do with a parade and fireworks?"

"We're scrambling to get things together. I think the most important thing is to have a bunch of us there when he gets off the plane. I know you'll be there."

"I will be if you pick me up. I'm standing outside my apartment and there's no Jeep."

"I'll take care of it. We're doubling up so we can all go and leave a car here for the volunteers we're bringing in to man the phones and take any calls."

"Sounds good. I'll see you when you get here."

But it wasn't Ernie driving her Jeep when she stepped outside her apartment. It was Nick. "This is Ernie's idea of a good time." He relinquished the steering wheel to her.

"You could've said no," she reminded him as she climbed in Jeep.

"I could have, but that would imply that there was

something wrong with being around you. That it bothered me in some way."

He looked out the side window as he spoke, never looking back at her. She sighed and started toward Main Street and the lovely old gingerbread houses that graced the heart of Diamond Springs. "Do you want me to drop you off at the hospital or at your place?"

"No, thanks. There was reason to this madness. Ernie told me about Joe, but my SUV is in the shop. I need a ride."

"Okay." She focused on her driving in a way she hadn't since she was sixteen and got her license the first time. She noticed every crack or bump in the street going out to the airport. Nick didn't say another word, just stared out the window at the passing scenery.

Sharyn couldn't stand it. She was used to talking to him about everything. "It will be good to have Joe back again."

"Yes it will."

"I'll bet Sarah and the girls have really missed him."

"I'm sure they did."

"Will we ever have any kind of normal relationship again?"

He glanced at her in surprise. "Define normal. Because I don't think we've ever had a normal relationship. You've always been busy being the sheriff and I've always been busy helping you."

"I meant a normal *personal* relationship." She knew

she was treading on dangerous ground, but something needed to be said. If they had any chance at all of reclaiming their relationship once Jack was in prison, they had to come to some sort of understanding.

"I don't think so. But I'm sure we can be great friends and have a wonderful working relationship."

"In other words, no."

"You know, I never realized how far the airport is from the city. Strange you don't notice those things."

She gave up. What did she expect anyway? That he would be eager and willing to make small talk? That he would pretend he wasn't angry and frustrated by her decision not to see him outside of work?

The problem was that she missed him. She missed his dry humor and surprising understanding of so many things. She missed not being able to pick up the phone and call him, knowing he was there for her.

But it might never be that way again. Even when she told him the truth, it might not matter.

They both took a deep breath as they pulled into the airport complex. It wasn't a big airport. Only small planes could land there. Big passenger jets landed in Charlotte or Raleigh. There were five or six hangars with several planes sitting on the tarmac outside of them. The sun made the white bodies gleam.

The tower was off in the distance, away from the terminal. Civilian passengers left or came in through the back of the building. Military passengers got off at a smaller green building near the tower. A high fence surrounded the complex, built for security in the last few years. Sharyn presented her badge to the guard at the gate. He waved her through along with Ernie and Ed behind her.

"That might be his plane." Nick pointed to the small military transport plane just landing.

"I hope in all our excitement to see Joe that someone thought about bringing Sarah and the girls."

Sharyn didn't have to worry. A good portion of Diamond Springs was already there with quickly made signs welcoming Joe and several other men and women home. Joe's wife and daughters were at the front of the pack with Trudy beside them.

She found a place to park and quickly joined the group, surprised to find Nick standing beside her. Ernie, Ed, Marvella, JP, and Cari came in after them. Everyone began yelling and crying as the door to the transport plane came down. The crowd surged forward, eager for a glance of a loved one's face. Many of the men and women returning home had been gone for nine months or more. Joe was lucky to have come back so quickly.

The delegation from the sheriff's department searched for Deputy Joe Landers' face in the group, not seeing him at first. Then he was there, coming off the ramp. He was being pushed in a wheelchair. His right leg was bandaged, but it was obvious that he had lost most of it.

The sign Sarah made fell to the ground. Sharyn and Ernie caught her as she followed it after calling her husband's name.

Chapter Six

"He didn't tell her," Sharyn said across Sarah's inert form.

"He didn't tell anyone, I guess." Ernie glanced at the other deputies as they rallied around Joe's young daughters who were crying and wondering what was wrong with their mother.

Sarah came around in a minute and picked herself up off the tarmac. "I'm okay. I don't want him to see me like this."

Sharyn helped her to her feet and brushed off the back of her skirt. "I can't believe he didn't say anything."

"That's Joe." Sarah smiled even though her lips trembled with the strain of not crying. She held her daughters close as her husband and his escort advanced on them.

Sharyn and Ernie stood in front of Sarah to give her a moment to pull herself together. The medic pushed Joe's wheelchair right up to them. Joe saluted him and smiled. "Thanks for the help." He grinned at his friends. "It's good to be home."

No one moved or said anything for a few seconds. Then Cari rushed forward and threw her arms around his neck. "It's good to have you home. Maybe now I can get a day off once in a while."

It broke the terrible tension. Everyone crowded around him as Sarah and the girls threw themselves on him. They cried and laughed at the same time. No one mentioned his leg, not making his homecoming a time to consider the future.

There was a problem getting the wheelchair into the back of Sarah's minivan, but Ernie and Ed managed it after putting their friend in the passenger seat.

Joe's smile was a thin line in his tense face. He was deeply tanned, except around the eyes where his ever-present sunglasses had protected his face from the hot Middle Eastern sun. Sharyn stood beside him as Sarah got in the driver's side while Nick and JP put some of his gear in the back.

"It's good to be home," he said again. "How have you been?"

"Fine." But Sharyn couldn't keep from saying, "You should've told us."

He looked at his hands. "I didn't know what to say. I thought if I could make it home, everything would work out."

"I'm sure it will. It's really good to see you. I think you could've used a little sunblock while you were gone."

"I'm light compared to some of them. I'm sorry I let everyone down by coming home so soon. My tour wasn't up, but they wouldn't let me stay."

"Good. We needed you back here anyway."

His dark eyes focused on hers. "It will never be the same."

"No. But it will be okay."

She closed the door and watched the green minivan drive away. Ernie stood beside her and shrugged. "Well, that's that," he said. "I guess we go back to the office."

It was a mutual, unspoken consent that kept them from talking about Joe yet. "Yeah. How's that going?"

"Good. Everything is getting back to normal. Don't worry about it. You just go on with your day off."

She nodded and walked back to where Nick was waiting. They got in the Jeep and headed for Diamond Springs. JP and Marvella followed them down the highway, veering off toward Main Street as they headed to the courthouse.

Sharyn stopped at the hospital to let Nick out. They

hadn't said a word to each other on the way back to town. She looked at him as he got out and turned around, hoping he wouldn't want to talk about Joe right now. She didn't think she could. As days off went, this one had proved to be full of unwelcome surprises. She just wanted to go home and get through the rest of the day.

"See you later," he said before he closed the door.

"You too," she whispered, turning away from him.

Sharyn went to dinner with Jack wearing an emerald-green velvet dress. She was careful with her hair, piling the copper-red curls on her head and securing them with a black barrette that Aunt Selma gave her for Christmas. She could tell Jack approved of the way she looked when his cold eyes brushed over her and he kissed her cheek.

The special event he'd promised turned out to be a gathering of all the prominent figures in the county. It was hosted by District Court Judge Tim Dailey at his estate that overlooked Diamond Mountain Lake.

All of the power brokers were there, sipping champagne with their elegantly dressed wives. Caison Talbot would have been here before his fall from grace. Mayor Todd Vance was there as well as *Diamond Springs Gazette* publisher, Jimmy Dalton. Judge Walter Hamilton and his wife, Ellen, were laughing as they spoke with George Albert, a county commissioner who had been a good friend of Sharyn's father.

These were the people who made everything happen in Diamond Springs. Sharyn looked at them as they ate caviar and gossiped. Did they all know Jack had paid to have her father killed? Did they discuss it like fluctuations in the stock market between bites of smoked salmon and brie?

She found herself standing on the outside of a heated debate between Jack and Judge Hamilton, trying to listen in on twenty different conversations, any one of which could mean trouble for the city.

Albert swept by at that moment and took her arm, urging her toward the open doors that led to the balcony. "What are you doing here, Sharyn?"

"I'm here with Jack." She didn't give anything away even though he was a family friend. Her mother wasn't too selective with her friends. As long as they were people with the right names and the right backgrounds, she was happy. Sharyn knew she couldn't trust anyone in that room.

"You shouldn't be here." He paced the balcony. The strong smell of cigar smoke followed him. "You're the sheriff. You're supposed to uphold the law, not help the people who break it."

"Then what are *you* doing here?" she demanded. "Are you one of the people who break the law? Why don't you do something about it if you know it's wrong?"

"It's not as easy as it sounds." He stared out at the lights around Diamond Lake. "I didn't want to be here. It happened over a period of years. Just like it did with your father."

She shivered in the cold, but wouldn't leave until she'd heard what he had to say. The FBI assured her that all of her questions about her father's reputation were unnecessary. He had worked with them for years trying to bring down the good-old-boys network, losing his life in the process. "Are you telling me my father did something illegal?"

"He didn't want to. He had no choice. They would have killed him. Possibly killed you or your mother too."

"They *did* kill him, George." She lost control of her temper. "As sure as I'm standing here. Did you think it was an accident he was gunned down in that convenience store?"

"You *know*?" He turned sharply to look at her. "Jack said—"

"I knew my ears were burning for a reason." Jack joined them. He reached a hand toward George. "Nice to see you. It's been a while. Congratulations on taking back your old commission seat. I'm sure you'll do a fine job for the town."

Sharyn couldn't see George's face in the darkness, but his voice sounded strained. "Thanks. It's good to be back. I've missed Diamond Springs."

"If you don't mind"—Jack took Sharyn's arm—"we're going inside for a while."

George agreed. *What else could he do?*

Sharyn went willingly with Jack. "Thanks for saving me."

"It was selfishness. I brought you here so we could spend time together while I butter up my benefactors. And I wanted them to see you with me as something more than the sheriff."

"This is definitely a who's who of Diamond Springs. The only one missing is Caison Talbot."

He laughed. "That's very perceptive of you! He would have been here before he forgot who he was and who the rest of us are. Too bad. Your mother would have fit in here."

"In that case, it's hard to believe I do."

He kissed the palm of her hand. "You fit in anywhere that I am."

"Thank you." She smiled at him. "I'm glad you think so."

"Of course, you know everyone here and everyone knows you. They know you as the sheriff now, but give them time to get used to seeing you without the badge. Someday, I hope to convince you to hang it up for good."

Sharyn didn't tell him she wasn't giving up being sheriff for him or anyone else. She sipped her sparkling water, smiled, and kept her own counsel. She knew what she wanted from this relationship even if no one else understood. They didn't have to. All she needed from them was to stay out of her way.

They walked around the room together. A few people eyed her suspiciously but she knew they wouldn't say anything. They were too afraid of alienating the man at her side. She wondered if Caison was ever king of the social heap like this. She wasn't sure what she was going to do if Jack or one of his friends asked for a special favor from the sheriff's department. Hopefully, if that happened, it would be the moment to pounce on Jack and all the rest of them.

Sharyn wondered what George was going to say to her on the balcony. She needed to try and get him alone, but not here. She'd always known he was part of this group. It seemed all of her father's friends were. No wonder everyone thought Jack corrupted him.

She was watching the door, wondering how long they were going to be there, when Nick came in. She almost choked on her water and put the glass down on the table nearby. *What are you doing here?* She wanted to tell him to leave before it was too late. She had sacrificed their relationship to keep him safe. If he got involved now, she couldn't protect him without giving everything away.

Sharyn tried to move into a corner of the room behind Judge Hamilton and his wife, but it was too late. Nick saw her and immediately walked toward her, a look of bedevilment on his lean, dark face.

All of the feelings of grief and heartache she'd had over telling him he couldn't be part of her life anymore bubbled up inside of her. She didn't want to face him with Jack looking on. She couldn't stand the idea of him gloating over taking her from Nick.

There was nowhere to go. The room was too crowded. Nick walked around Judge Hamilton with a casual word for the people near him and stood beside Sharyn in the small alcove. "I knew I'd find you here. How's life with Diamond Springs' elite?"

"What are you doing here?"

His back was to the room as he faced her. "What are *you* doing here?"

"I'm here with Jack." She raised her chin a notch. They were of an equal height, gazes glaring into each other's faces.

"Of course you are." His voice was low and rasping. "And the moon is made of cheese. Do you think everyone here is stupid? You don't think they all know *exactly* why you're here?"

Did he really know?

"Jack finds me attractive and I find him attractive." She wasn't going to admit anything.

"Jack is looking for a way to play you just like he tried to do with your father. Just like he tries to do with everyone. He might find you attractive, but only in the evil, power broker kind of way."

He didn't know.

"Go home." Relieved, she turned away from him and looked around the room.

"Not without you."

"I'm *not* leaving."

"Then neither am I." He leaned against the wall beside her.

She wasn't sure what to do. She hadn't expected this and didn't know how to deal with it. Nick had respected her decision to break up with him with his usual brand of sarcasm and flair for annoying her.

They weren't at a crime scene where she could walk away or even at her apartment where she could close the door. She was afraid he was going to ruin everything.

She closed her eyes and opened them again to see him staring at her. "You need to go. Please."

"Why? I paid my hundred dollars to be here raising campaign money for our dear senator. I have a right to be here."

"Now isn't the time to be stupid and stubborn."

"Are you afraid you can't stand the competition for those categories?"

Jack joined them, looking from Nick to Sharyn and back again. "Is there a problem?"

"It all depends on how you look at it," Nick said. "I have to borrow your date for a while."

Sharyn and Jack both turned to question him. Jack got his words in first. "Get over it, Doc. She made her choice."

Not able to handle the stricken look on Nick's face, Sharyn added, "It's business, Jack. Nick has some news about Michaelson's death."

Jack smiled in an ugly, mean way. "I thought we agreed you weren't going to investigate that, darling."

"Get over it, Senator," Nick returned. "She has no choice. A suicide is a homicide until I say different."

"And are you saying Michaelson's death wasn't a suicide?" Jack glared at him, daring him to say it wasn't.

"That's between me and the sheriff right now." Nick nodded at Sharyn. "I'll meet you at the morgue."

She agreed, not sure what they were talking about. She thought she was making up a plausible excuse for Nick's appearance at Jack's fundraiser. Maybe she was wrong. Maybe he *was* looking for her because he learned something about Michaelson. She felt stupid thinking he was there for a more personal reason. The problem with Nick was that she was never really sure.

She watched him leave, careful not to follow his movements too closely for fear Jack would notice. This one moment could make or break Jack's belief in her. She had to go on with the path she'd chosen.

Jack excused himself for a moment. She watched him talk to a man she'd never seen before. She wished she had one of those small spy cameras that James Bond always carried. If she had a picture of him, she could feed it into the FBI database and see what came up. This way all she could do was memorize his features. There was nothing unusual about him. Medium height, medium build, bad suit.

He glanced around the room and nodded before he and Jack separated. She watched him go over by the punch bowl as Jack came back to her side.

"Nick is a strange man," Jack said. "I never know how to take him."

She shrugged. "He's from New York. No one from the south ever knows how to take someone from New York."

He laughed. "That's true. I don't understand what you saw in him. He's a little morose, isn't he?"

"I think it was a work thing." She looked away from him as she spoke. The man Jack had spoken to was gone. She glanced around the room but didn't see him anywhere. A chill crept down her spine and she shivered.

Jack put his hand on her arm. "Goose cross your grave?"

"I think so." She smiled at the old term. "I have to go powder my nose."

"Do you have to leave?"

"Not yet. Whatever Nick has to say can wait. Everything is an emergency with him. I'll be right back."

Sharyn walked confidently through the room, smiling and holding her head up. She didn't feel that way inside. The deception cut across her grain. She hoped Jack, or one of his friends, would mess up quickly so she could get this over with.

There were other women in the elegant bathroom. They laughed and talked about their children and their soccer games. One was expecting a new diamond bracelet for her birthday. Another was expecting a new car.

Ellen Albert, George's wife, was sitting silently looking at herself in the large, ornate mirror. Sharyn knew her well from childhood. Ellen had great parties even though Sharyn disliked going to them because their son, Richard, was a bully.

Ellen looked as though she'd been crying. Sharyn took her time washing her hands and checking her hair, waiting until the other women were gone before she sat down beside Ellen on the striped chaise. "Are you all right?" she asked her mother's friend.

"I don't know what that means," Ellen answered in a listless voice.

"Is there anything I can do for you?"

She stared at Sharyn in the mirror. "Get us both out of here?"

"I can take you home if George wants to stay."

"That's not what I mean." Ellen shook her head. "I didn't want to come back here. Not with what happened . . ."

"No one holds that against you or George," Sharyn maintained. "What happened, happened. This is still your home."

Ellen grasped Sharyn's hand. "You don't see. Don't

get involved in this. I didn't want to come back because I knew George would be in the thick of things like he was before. He always said it was for Richard, but I knew the truth. And here we are again."

"Tell me about it." Sharyn hoped this unexpected source could help her.

"I can't. George is all I have. They'd kill him."

Sharyn squeezed her hand. "I can protect him. I know people who could help him."

"They *know* those people too, bless your heart. George can't walk away now. Before, we had a chance. Now we're stuck. No one can help us."

Olivia Dalton stuck her head around the door. "We're almost ready for the big announcement, Ellen. What are you doing in here, Sharyn? I think Jack is looking for you."

Ellen smiled and patted Sharyn's hand. "She was giving me a hand with my hair. When it gets humid, I have a problem with it staying up." She smiled at Sharyn and got to her feet. Her eyes were still wet with tears. "Thank you, darlin'. You were always a sweet girl."

The two older women went out and Sharyn tried to get over her disappointment. Every time she thought she might have a lead into the truth, something happened to it. She might be ninety before she found out what she needed to know. Her life would be over, but she would know the truth about what happened to her father.

She stared at her reflection in the mirror. She didn't want that for her life, but she was dedicated to getting to the heart of the cancer that ate at their town. She was going to cut that heart out of this group.

When she got back to the ballroom, the band was striking up announcement music. Jack was standing on a platform at the front of the room with the others looking up at him like he was king. Sharyn didn't know what to expect. He'd given her no idea anything momentous was going to happen, but apparently that was why he wanted her here.

"I want to say thanks to everyone who's here tonight." He waited until the fanfare died down. "You all know me. You know I've been alone in my struggles for a long time. But not anymore."

He looked down at Sharyn and she wondered if it was too late to run and hide. She had a bad feeling about this suddenly. She didn't like the way he was looking at her.

"You know I'm getting ready to begin my senatorial campaign again. I appreciate all of your help and support down through the years. We all know there is only one thing that could put me in better standing for this race. My opponent doesn't know anything about what it takes to fill a senate seat. I'm not worried about that."

The room filled with laughter at his humor. Sly glances that slid Sharyn's way made her feel like Mia Farrow in *Rosemary's Baby*. She knew she wasn't about to have the son of the devil, but she felt like she was consorting with him.

"I'm talking about my personal life, of course. Nothing makes a politician more vulnerable than a character debate. But I think I've found the answer to that issue." He looked out at the audience then held his hand out for Sharyn to join him on the platform. "Sharyn Howard has graciously agreed to be my wife. And I am humbly grateful to have the sheriff of Montgomery County on my team."

The applause covered Sharyn's feelings of horror and entrapment. What had she done? She took Jack's hand and stood beside him, smiling and wondering if there was any way out of this. She could see where he'd been leading since the beginning. Nick was right. She and Agent Brewster believed Jack was attracted to her and she could use that to find a weak spot.

Instead, he planned to use her to further his career. The only thing she really had was her reputation and her family's name. But that was what he wanted. He wanted to parade her around while he ran for the senate.

Jack held her hand in his and kissed the side of her mouth. Thunderous applause erupted in the room. Sharyn's face was stretched from smiling at all of Jack's supporters.

What could she do? She could walk out now and leave him flat. That would kill the investigation, but save her sanity. She could stay and put off his marriage plans and hope she would find something to put him in prison before she had to say "I do."

She was never taking another day off. Between learning about Joe, lunch with her aunt and finding out Jack had marriage plans, it was better for her to work forever. Maybe that was the only thing keeping unpleasant surprises at bay.

"I hope you aren't angry I sprang that information on you," Jack said as the party continued around them.

Sharyn thought fast and took her hand from him. "I didn't want to embarrass you in front of your friends, but I need time to consider this. I don't appreciate you putting me on the spot."

There was a long moment when she wasn't sure what he'd say. She was taking her chances that he'd expect some kind of response from her. If she was wrong and he expected her to be completely compliant, she was dead in the water.

He put his head back and laughed. "I wouldn't expect less from you. That's one of the things I find most attractive about you, Sharyn. You're not a yes man. Or woman, in this case. Take all the time you need, but I'd like to plan a June wedding. I've already spoken with Faye and Caison. They are both thrilled."

Right. Sharyn smiled, thinking this was what predicated the terrible lunch with Aunt Selma. They knew

Jack's plans before she did. That was why they were trying to warn her off. *Why didn't they just come out and say it? Did everything have to be a mystery?*

"We'll see," she said to Jack. "I need to go now. I have to work tomorrow. It's getting late."

"Of course, that would be one of the benefits of being my wife. You could hang Jacob's old gun up for good."

Sharyn thought about that as the limousine driver swept through the quiet streets of Diamond Springs on the way back to her apartment. Jack had decided to stay on at the party. No doubt plenty of dealings he would rather her not know about until he was sure of her loyalty. Would it take a wedding to prove that to him?

She hoped not. He wouldn't need her after the election and she could prove to be a liability to him. She could get too close if they lived together. Of course, if he could get her to give up being sheriff, he could continue to trade on her name and connections.

She closed and locked her door when she got home and immediately tried to call Agent Brewster on her cell phone to let him know what happened. She didn't dare use her land line. They already knew Jack had it tapped. She only discussed trivial family matters on that line.

Brewster didn't answer his phone. He never did. She left him a message, hoping he would want to set up a meeting. They usually met somewhere in the mountains. She could use a good hike to clear her mind.

Talking to Brewster made her feel like she wasn't in the *Twilight Zone*. He was the only contact she had with the real world. He wasn't much in the comfort or advice department, but it was another human being to talk to about the situation. He usually nodded and told her they were getting closer to bringing Jack down. She wasn't sure it was true, but it was better than nothing.

Sharyn changed clothes. She was sorry she'd worn the emerald gown. She'd bought it last year to wear some place special and impress Nick. Now it was tainted. She wouldn't do anything dramatic like burning it, although it seemed like a good idea. Instead, it would probably hang in her closet for a few years until she gave it to some charity. She would certainly never wear it again.

Of course, she might not need to. As a senator's wife, she'd have way too many evening gowns and cocktail dresses.

She looked at herself in her jeans, T-shirt and flannel over-shirt. Her hair was loose and curly on her shoulders, the deep red highlights glinting in the bathroom light. Blue eyes like her father's and her aunt's stared back at her.

The investigation was important to her. Bringing Jack down was important to her. *But I won't marry him.* The souls she wanted to bring closure for would have to understand she couldn't go that far. She didn't know about David, but she knew her father wouldn't ask that of her. Somehow, she and Brewster had to find a way to get at Jack before June.

Sharyn sat down with her laptop to take a look at Jack's opponents for his senate seat. She typed in the address of the Montgomery County Board of Election website. She knew there was a primary in May, but hadn't paid much attention to who was running. She scrolled down at the site and looked at who was registered.

Jack's name was there, of course. But there was a surprise challenger from his party who would have run against him in the primary. "Alan Michaelson. What made you think you stood a chance of taking Jack on?"

So there was possible motive behind what happened. It seemed like overkill to her. Unless Michaelson really lost it and decided to take his girlfriend out, setting him up to take the fall for Michelle's death would have been all that was necessary to quell his political ambitions. Why kill him?

Maybe Jack wasn't involved with that. Maybe Michaelson was either guilty or realized what he was in store for and killed himself. Either way, it was a possible link to Jack, especially since he happened to be in town today. It seemed unusual that he would get his hands dirty that way, but maybe he wanted to be sure the job was done right.

She looked for his opponent from the other party.

There was only one person running which would explain why there was no primary coverage. Sharyn sat forward and almost dropped her laptop when she read the name. *Selma Howard-Two-Rivers.*

Chapter Seven

"Why didn't you tell me?" Sharyn demanded of Selma the next morning. She followed her aunt around the kitchen in the old Howard homestead about five miles outside Diamond Springs.

As soon as Sam saw the look on Sharyn's face, he retreated to the basement. Selma was in the middle of making pies for a charity bake sale and didn't seem to mind Sharyn's tirade.

"What would be the point talking about it?" Selma took two apple pies out of the oven and put two more in. Already the top of her wooden table was covered in nicely browned pies. "You can't talk me out of it and, truly, talking to you at all is like sleeping with the enemy."

"Did *anyone* try to talk you out of it?" Sharyn asked. "Did anyone say what a stupid thing this is to do?"

Selma paused briefly to look at her. "I love you, but don't tell me I'm stupid. I won't tolerate *that* from anyone."

Sharyn sat down and stared at the pies. "I'm sorry. I'm just worried about you. We both know what Jack is capable of doing. We all know he killed Trudy's husband and David. I don't want anything to happen to you."

"What are you talking about?" It was Selma's turn to confront her niece. "You *are* going to marry him. You're dating him or whatever it is they call it now. How can you say those things about him? You gave up *Nick* to be with him."

A thousand excuses rattled through Sharyn's brain. She could feel the impact of Selma's direct gaze even without looking at her. She was going to have to make what she said believable. "It's different with me and him. I don't expect you to understand. Jack loves me. I think we're good together."

Selma shook her head. "And you're calling *me* stupid?" She turned away to continue working on another half dozen pies on the counter. "If you weren't grown up, I'd take you over my knee. I'm tempted to anyway. Where's your good sense, child? He's using you. He's using the Howard name and your reputation to fight me for the senate seat. He knows it's the only chance he has. And if he can corrupt you along the way, so much the better."

"He doesn't want to corrupt me," Sharyn denied. "I know his games. He doesn't play them with me."

"Someone must have hit you in the head with something and scrambled your brains." Selma threw a copy of the *Diamond Springs Gazette* into her lap. On the front page was a picture of Sharyn and Jack. The article was about their engagement and forthcoming wedding. "And I suppose you plan to go through with this?"

Sharyn stared at the picture. "You don't understand, Aunt Selma. He's different than he seems. He means a lot to me."

"He's going to destroy you."

"You'll see after the wedding." Sharyn forced a cheerful, brainless smile to her face even though the effort left a bad taste in her mouth. "We're going to make a great couple."

"I think I was wrong." Selma set two cherry pies to bake. "You aren't stupid. You're crazy. If you sleep with the devil, some of his evil will be with you forever. Your father, bless his soul, learned about Jack the hard way. Go visit him in the churchyard and tell him about your brilliant wedding."

"Aunt Selma, I know what I'm doing."

"Does it include ruining your life? Or does it only include ruining the life of the man you really love? Jack is no better than a rattlesnake in the barn. An easy solution would be to take your grandfather's gun and shoot him between the eyes."

"I wish you wouldn't talk like that. Can't you just wish me well?"

"At what cost, Sharyn? I lost my first love because of Jack. I lost your father. I won't lose you."

Sharyn tried to go back to their original conversation. "But I don't know if I can protect you from Jack if you run against him. He'd do almost anything for me but he's very competitive."

Selma smiled. "Listen to you! Is there an alien inside of you? What you're saying isn't making any sense. You love Jack. He loves you. You're afraid he might kill me to keep his senate seat. The real Sharyn Howard can't be inside of you."

Sharyn got to her feet. "I have to go to work. I love you. I don't want to fight with you. I'll do what I can to keep you safe. I'm glad you and Sam are together now. He can watch your back."

Selma hugged her. "I love you too. Please be careful. Don't let this go too far. He'll ruin you. I don't want to visit you in the churchyard at your father's side."

"Good morning!" Faye Howard joined them with Caison in tow carrying pies. "Sharyn! It's good to see you! We haven't seen each other in weeks. Let's plan to have lunch." Sharyn's mother patted her neat straw hat on her blond head. She was about six inches shorter than her daughter, petite, and always well dressed. Today her country look included a pink-and-white-checked dress under her neat pink coat.

Sharyn hugged her mother and promised to call her when she had free time. She stopped and nodded at Caison, not quite willing to hug him yet. Maybe not ever. She explained that she had to go and left the couple in the warm, fragrant kitchen with Selma.

When the door closed behind her, Faye laughed and clapped her hands. "Did you see Sharyn with Jack in the paper today? I may have grandchildren yet."

Sam came up from the basement, exchanging glances with Caison and Selma.

Selma retied her apron and took the half-baked pies from her sister-in-law. "Excuse me if I don't blubber over Sharyn marrying a man so much older than her and a criminal to boot."

Faye stared at her then turned to Caison. "Selma has always been a little strange. But we love her anyway."

Sharyn drove back to Diamond Springs and got a mocha latte to go at the diner across the street from the courthouse. She had to wait for traffic to get back to the pink granite building, an unheard of thing until the last few years.

Bringing the interstate highway from Charlotte to Diamond Springs brought greater prosperity to the area than anyone had ever dreamed of. It also brought overcrowded schools, more crime, and not as many tax dollars as the county needed to handle it. A little more money trickled in every year, but the state withheld a little more each year so it became a balancing act for Montgomery County to survive the onslaught.

The new sheriff's office was a victim to that issue. It lost funding twice due to other capitol improvements that were more desperately needed. It was back on schedule now, but what mattered to her was still trudging to the basement of the courthouse for the day.

Trudy was already at work, her mouth drawn in a thin line of disapproval. Sharyn realized she would be arguing about her relationship with Jack all day. It had been difficult to lie to Selma. Lying to Trudy and Ernie was just as hard. She'd known them her entire life. She knew what they were thinking about her and Jack. She had to follow her plan to protect them as much as to destroy Jack.

There was someone in her office reporting to Jack. The journal she'd accidentally discovered in the old office hinted at her father facing the same predicament. He'd believed someone on his staff was giving away information. For a long time Sharyn believed it was David. He'd worked with her father before her. His death, and the fact that he was working with the FBI, cleared his good name.

By the same token, she refused to believe it was Trudy, Ed, Joe, or Ernie. She cringed to think it could be one of the deputies she'd hired: Cari, Marvella, JP, or Terry. She didn't want to believe any of them could be guilty of working with Jack.

"Good morning," Sharyn said to Trudy before she got her mail.

"Is it?" Trudy didn't look back at her, her thin shoulders stiff and unyielding like her judgment.

"Don't start with me, I've already had it from Selma, Sam, and Caison."

"Caison? That's like the pot calling the kettle black!"

"Exactly. So you can see what I'm up against."

Before Trudy could say anything else, the phone rang and Ernie came into the office. He took off his hat and jacket then sat beside Sharyn.

She smiled at him. "You look terrible."

He ran his hand through the single sprig of hair on his head. There were dark circles under his eyes and deep lines that spoke of him not sleeping. "I was with Joe most of the night. Ed was there too. I don't know what we're going to do. He's a mess."

Sharyn had tried to avoid thinking about it as much as she could. There was no other answer. "We can offer him a desk job. It's all we can do. We're not in a position to make any other call. He can't work the way he did before."

"Don't you think I know that? Even worse, *he* knows that. His life is over."

"Don't be stupid. He'll get a prosthetic and he'll learn to use it. Not every job is as physically demanding as being a sheriff's deputy. He'll learn to do something else."

"He doesn't *want* to do something else. And he won't take a desk job."

"There's nothing else we can do. How is he besides that?"

"He's pretty good. He'll need a lot of therapy, but I think he'll survive." Ernie opened his eyes. "Do you want to put an ad out to look for another deputy?"

"I guess we'll have to. I have to get the okay from the commission first. I'll try to keep them open on letting Joe stay at a desk job."

"Get Mr. Percy involved if you have to," Ernie snarled. "Joe is supposed to be guaranteed his job when he comes back from serving his country. Mr. Percy won't let them run over a vet."

Sharyn nodded. "Is that it? How are we standing on the hit and run?"

"Nick found that the paint from Michaelson's Humvee matched the paint we found on the body. Michaelson, or someone driving his vehicle, hit that girl. Lucky thing she left the little boy in the van or he'd be dead too."

"Did his daddy take him home from the hospital yet?"

"Last I heard, they still had him there. I don't see any reason to throw suspicion on the aunt and the father at this point. Despite their relationship, I don't think they were involved."

"It just worked out nicely for them, huh?"

"I guess so. Like you and Jack. I hear congratulations are in order." Ernie's dark eyes were filled with questions and plenty of other things he wanted to say to her.

"Thanks. It came up unexpectedly." Sharyn was glad he kept those comments to himself.

Ed came in as they were talking. He poured himself a cup of coffee as he winked at Trudy from across the room. She smiled in response and answered the phone.

"Morning." He sat down close to Sharyn and Ernie. The revelation about Joe's injury and the long night had taken their toll on him as well. His pretty-boy face looked haggard and drawn. "So, what's the verdict?"

Joe and Ed had been partners for as long as anyone could remember. Sharyn looked at him and realized he knew the answer before he asked. "I'm sorry. We can only offer him a desk job."

"I guess I knew that. With all the newfangled gadgets in the world, why can't they make a leg for a man that will work like the real thing?"

"We'll have to look for someone else," Ernie said. "Since he or she will be your partner, we'll let you sit in on the process."

Ed smiled and shook his head. "I've been thinking about that, old son. I think it might be time for me to move on. I've still got a few years until retirement to work. Maybe I'll learn another trade. I've been doing this since I got out of high school and T. Raymond recruited me. Now I think it might be best for me to do something else."

Ernie stared at him. "Don't be stupid. You know you don't want to do anything else."

"Maybe not, but I sure don't want to break in a new partner."

Sharyn considered it. "How about if we bring Terry from the night shift to be your partner? You two seem to get along. Then we'll hire the new person to work nights."

Ed shrugged. "That might work. I'll have to think about it." He got to his feet. "I guess the whole thing with David and now with Joe has gotten to me. Everybody tries not to let things bother them, but I'm really bothered right now."

Ernie stood up beside him and clapped him on the shoulder. David Matthews was Ed's nephew. He was the one who got the boy on the job in the first place. "It's not so much what's past as where you're going. I know you. We grew up together. You wouldn't know what to do with yourself and then you'd drive Trudy crazy and she'd kick you out. What kind of life would that be?"

Ed laughed. "I guess you're right. Terry might be okay to work with. He's a good boy."

Sharyn was glad Ed reconsidered. It was bad enough to lose Joe. She didn't want to think about trying to replace both of them. It wasn't just the fact that the department would be down two deputies. It was their place in her life. They were more like family than people she worked with. "What's up for this morning?" she asked Ernie.

He checked the schedule. "You're due at a budget meeting with the county commission at two P.M. Ed is testifying in court today. Who knows how long that will take? We should hear something from Nick about Michaelson's death. I guess if he calls it a homicide, we'll be investigating that crime scene further."

"What about our hit-and-run victim?" Sharyn asked. "I know the paint from Michaelson's Hummer matches the paint on her. Are we sure Michaelson was driving that vehicle?"

Ernie scribbled some notes on his clipboard. "I'll check that out."

"Put it on the schedule for second shift," she told him. "With Ed in court and me at the commission, we need you free for calls. Let Marvella and JP handle it."

"Okay. But it gets dark pretty early. They'll have to go out right away."

"Have Trudy give them a call and let them know what's going on." She got to her feet. "I have someone I need to talk to before lunch. Call me if you hear from Nick."

Ernie agreed. He was about to speak when Trudy took a nine-one-one call from a twelve-year-old boy who was home alone and heard noises in the basement. He looked at Sharyn, changed his mind, and pushed his hat down on his head before going outside.

"That man has a lot on his mind," Ed said. "I'm surprised his head doesn't explode."

"The only thing he's got in his brain today," Sharyn said, "is telling me how to live my life."

Ed shrugged. "Well, sometimes you need a little advice, you know?"

"Not you too!" She picked up her jacket. "I better go now before *my* head explodes."

"I think somebody needs to talk some sense into you," Trudy added between calls. "I just don't know what's wrong with your mama. She should be the one straightening you out."

Sharyn laughed. "Instead, she's the only one who loved the picture in the paper."

Trudy glanced up at her. "There was a picture in the paper?"

Putting on her brown uniform jacket, Sharyn left the conversation and walked outside. She blinked in the bright sunlight, automatically putting on her sunglasses. Despite the sunshine, the wind coming down from the mountains was cold. She pulled up the collar on her jacket and walked out to her Jeep.

She was meeting Agent Brewster at the state park entrance on Diamond Mountain. The park was closed this time of year, but everyone knew the small cabin by the gate was left open. Hikers were discouraged from tackling the mountain in the winter time, but that didn't always stop them. The cabin was an emergency shelter for them.

It was a good place to meet. The area was isolated now. In the summer and fall it was full of visitors. Only the occasional stray animal or crazy extreme snowboarder might be likely to wander in now. She could keep her eye on that. Any place else, in town or out in the county, was too risky. All it took was a wrong move or a wrong word for this whole scheme to come crashing down on her.

Sometimes she thought that might be for the best. She'd wished it was over even before it began. Now she felt trapped, not sure where she was going. She had to find a way to end this before Aunt Selma's words of warning came true.

Agent Brewster's gray Ford Explorer was waiting at the side of the cabin. The gate across the road that led up the mountain and into the park was chained closed, but Sharyn could see tire tracks beyond the gate. She stared up at the craggy face of the mountain, indentations of white snow still crisscrossing the highest peaks. There was no way to tell if those tracks belonged to a ranger or someone out joy riding. She was going to have to let someone else handle it.

She parked her Jeep beside the Explorer and glanced around the area. There was no one out there that she could see. She always felt a little nervous when she met Brewster. After years of being a recognizable public figure, it made her uneasy trying to sneak around.

Brewster got up from trying to coax a fire to life in the one room cabin. He automatically glanced beyond Sharyn as she walked in the door, years of habit watching out for the unexpected. He took off his gloves and held his hand out to her. "Glad you could make it. Are things clearing up in the county now?"

"Pretty much. There are a few scattered power outages. Those always cause their own problems. Otherwise, we seem to be okay."

"I heard about your deputy." He nodded. "Tough break."

His tone put Sharyn's hackles up. She didn't really like Agent Brewster. She supposed she trusted him. She didn't have much choice. She wasn't sure if it was her southern upbringing or the fact that her mother raised her to be polite, but Brewster had an obnoxious disregard for most common courtesies.

"I suppose you could call it that," she said. "He won't be able to work as a deputy again, at least not the way he's used to. Most people I know would call that more than a tough break."

"Sorry." He half-smiled at her. "I didn't mean to make light of it."

She shook her head. "It doesn't matter. I suppose you've heard that there has been movement with Jack."

"Yes. What went on at the party last night?"

Sharyn named the guests and told him everything that happened while she was there. She explained about the engagement and Jack announcing it without telling her.

"He's pretty certain of you," Brewster said. "That's good. He probably trusts you out of arrogance, if nothing else. That's a good place for him to make a mistake."

"He wants to be married in June."

"How romantic!"

"I think that means we better move quickly. I'm not changing my name to his."

"I can't say I blame you there. But don't get too impatient or we'll lose him. We may never have another chance like this."

Sharyn stepped to the window to look out at the mountain that had always provided her with inspiration. "Isn't there something I can do to force the issue?"

"Nothing that I can think of right now. Just hang in there and wait for the right moment. You're an officer of the law. All you need him to do is step over the line. If he forgets for one minute who you are or thinks what you see doesn't matter, you've got him."

Sharyn told him about Michaelson and Jack's timely visit. "He told me not to bother investigating any further. Could your men do a sweep of the house? My boys are really pushed to the limit."

Brewster considered the matter. "I'll see what I can do, but if Nick decides it isn't a suicide, you'll have to investigate. You can always tell Jack it will look suspicious not to."

"I'll check into that angle. Nick was at the party last night for a few minutes. He said he had something, but I haven't heard anything else from him."

"You think it was just a reason to talk to you? Have you told him the truth?"

"No." She looked back at him. "I didn't want to take a chance by telling him what I was doing."

"I still think that's best. This way everyone knows the two of you are history and Nick's performance is convincing."

There it was again. It felt like someone jabbing at her with a pencil. "I don't think it's a performance. Maybe I'm being vain, but I think he really loved me."

"Maybe. If so, it could work out for you when this is all over and you are the county heroine."

Sharyn didn't want to hear anymore. She only *thought* Aunt Selma's lectures were bad. "I better go. I'll let you know if anything else happens."

"Fine. Remember to let me know if you think something is coming up. The court will most likely respect the fact that you're a sheriff, but there's nothing like hearing it too. I'd like you to wear a wire if it comes down to it."

She agreed and let herself out of the cabin, looking around before she got in her Jeep. She was backing out to turn around when the call came in.

"Sheriff, we've had a break-in and assault at the hospital." Trudy's voice was less than steady over the radio.

"What happened? Is Ernie on his way over there?"

"Ernie is over there already. So are Ed and Marvella."

"Marvella?" Sharyn felt her heart beat a little faster. "What's she doing in already?"

"Ernie thought we might need her. It's Nick, Sharyn.

Someone broke into the morgue. Ernie said the place is a mess."

"And Nick?"

"I don't know. He was unconscious. They sent some-one down to take him to the emergency room. I can't even think about it after this thing with Joe. Nick has to be okay."

Sharyn knew where her duty lay in this. Still she fought with herself all the way to Diamond Springs with the blue light flashing, siren screaming.

She knew she had to go to the morgue. It was the crime scene. But the more she thought about Nick be-ing hurt, possibly seriously injured, the more she knew she couldn't do her duty until she knew he was okay.

Trudy said they took him to the emergency room. It was on the back side of the hospital. The morgue was to the right, in the basement. Sharyn swung the Jeep to the back parking lot, and for once, took advantage of the fact that she was the sheriff. She turned off the lights and siren, shut off the engine and left the Jeep parked almost sideways at the entrance to the emergency room.

"You can't park there," a young intern told her as she passed him on the sidewalk.

"I'm the sheriff," she yelled as she passed him. "I can park wherever I want."

She didn't care what he thought of that sentiment.

All that mattered was finding out if Nick was okay. She remembered the time at Bell's Creek when the old cabin collapsed on her. He was there when she woke up. He was always there when she needed him. *How could I push him aside this way? Is any revenge worth living without him? What if he dies and I never have a chance to tell him the truth?*

She plunged into the empty waiting room, looking for someone who could point her in the right direction. She realized she was breathing hard and probably looked a little wild-eyed. She forced herself to take a few deep breaths and calm down. She had to look like the sheriff; cool, objective and in control.

A nurse in green scrubs came around the corner. "Can I help you?"

"I'm looking for Nick Thomopolis. He was brought in a few minutes ago."

"Are you a relative?"

Sharyn wanted to yell at her, but she kept it businesslike. "I'm the sheriff. I'm here on a case."

"Sorry, Sheriff. Let me check for you. I just came on duty." The woman smiled and went behind the counter to look at the computer. "I see that Dr. Thomopolis was brought in from downstairs. He was attacked here at the hospital?" The woman shook her head. "What is this world coming to?"

"Where is he?" Sharyn didn't bother with any conversational pleasantries.

"He's in the exam room, but he's scheduled for some tests in a few minutes. Maybe you should wait—"

"Where's the exam room?"

"Through those doors. Maybe I should have the doctor speak to you." The woman picked up the phone.

"Thanks." Sharyn walked through the doors and left the woman standing with the phone in her hand.

The back exam area was as empty as the front waiting area. Maybe people went to their own doctor's office during the day, she considered, as she glanced into each of the exam rooms.

"Excuse me." A man who was dressed in green scrubs stopped her. "Can I help you?"

"I'm looking for Nick Thomopolis. He's the medical examiner and he was brought in a few minutes ago."

"Yes. I'm Dr. Lazar, the physician on duty." He looked at her uniform. "Are you going to arrest him for something, Deputy?"

"I'm Sheriff Sharyn Howard. I want to see Nick Thomopolis *now.*"

The doctor glanced at her in a curious way, but didn't attempt to argue with her. "Come this way."

Sharyn followed him, glad he didn't pursue his questioning. Her few moments of calm detachment were almost over. If she didn't see Nick alive and breathing soon, she was going to lose whatever self-control she had mustered.

Dr. Lazar pushed aside a curtain in the corner of the

large exam room. Nick was lying on the bed, his eyes closed. His face was bruised and swollen. There was a cut above one eye and at the corner of his mouth.

Sharyn put one hand on the side of the bed to keep from dropping on the floor. How many times had she seen death and serious injuries without feeling this way? It was like she wasn't the sheriff anymore. She was a helpless woman who didn't know what to do in the face of pain and suffering. "How is he?"

"We aren't sure yet. We're going to do a MRI in a few minutes to be sure there are no internal injuries. I'm sure he has a concussion, some bruises and lacerations. Until he regains consciousness, we won't know the extent of the damage."

She asked him about following forensic protocol in a voice that sounded hollow and scared to her ears. He replied that a deputy was with them when they first examined Nick and had taken his clothes for further study. Sharyn glanced at him as he spoke, guessing she sounded normal to him. She focused on saying the right things and keeping herself standing. It might be all right to fall on the floor and cry if she *wasn't* the sheriff and trying to look professional, but she *was* the sheriff. She had to hold it together.

When the doctor told her everything he knew about Nick's injuries, he excused himself to be sure the MRI was being readied for his patient. "You can stay here, if you like, until they take him down."

"Thanks." She didn't look away from Nick's face. "I appreciate your help."

"You know, there probably isn't a person in this hospital that doesn't know Nick was dating the sheriff. You don't have to try so hard to impress me."

Sharyn didn't reply. When Dr. Lazar closed the curtain behind him as he left, she stepped closer to the bed. She put her hand carefully against Nick's chest and felt tears well in the back of her eyes.

She didn't want to hurt him, but she needed to be close to him, if only for a moment before they came to get him. She said a small prayer of thanks that they were taking him for an MRI instead of taking him back down to the morgue. He could've been dead. She might have been too late.

Carefully, she lowered her head beside his, wiping tears away before they fell on him. She closed her eyes as she brushed her cheek against his. "I'm so sorry. I love you, Nick. I didn't know what I was doing. I'm so glad you're alive."

He sighed and shifted painfully on the hospital bed. "The things a man has to do to get a woman these days."

Chapter Eight

"You're *awake*?" she demanded angrily, moving away from him though one hand still lingered on his chest.

"I wasn't until someone started dribbling water on me." He opened his eyes and looked at her. "Oh. It was you. Are you *crying*?"

"No." She sniffed and wiped her eyes with her hands. "Yes. What happened?"

"I don't think I can talk about that yet." He touched a finger to her face.

She nodded. "Post shock syndrome. You'll be fine later."

"I don't think I'm *past* the shock yet. Did you say all

those things to me because you thought I was unconscious? I thought it was over between us."

"We shouldn't talk about that right now," she replied briskly. "You're seriously injured. You should rest. Don't talk."

"You were ready enough to hear about how this happened," he reminded her. "Don't run away because it gets personal."

Sharyn was still crying. She couldn't seem to stop. She grabbed a handful of tissues from the bedside table. "I'm glad you're okay. I think it's this whole thing after finding out about Joe. It's been a bad week."

He stared at her. "Jack announced your engagement."

"I know." She blew her nose. "I should go. They want to take you down for some tests. We can talk later."

"No, we can't." He reached for her hand.

She couldn't help it. She slipped her hand into his. "This is stupid. I should go."

"Do you or don't you love me?"

"It doesn't matter. Not now."

"It matters to me. As angry as I'm going to be if you tell me you are insanely plotting some kind of downfall for Jack by pretending you want to marry him, I think I can live with that better than knowing you don't love me."

Sharyn was torn, wishing they would come up there

and take Nick away. It was bad enough that she was here, crying all over him. She couldn't give away her plan. But when she looked into his dark eyes, she knew she had to tell him the truth. She could have lost him forever. Even if it meant not finding out the truth about Jack, she had to tell Nick how she felt.

"I love you," she whispered. "I never stopped loving you."

He tugged on her hand until she bent down close to him. "I love you too. But I am *really* angry that you did this to us. I wish I could say I'm surprised, but I'm not. Sharyn, you can't help your father, David, or anyone else by destroying your own life."

"I'm sorry. I'd like to say it was all Agent Brewster's idea, but it wouldn't be true. I wanted to do whatever it took to get Jack. I still do."

"What about us?"

"Us?" She stared at him in disbelief. "Is there still an 'us?' "

"As long as I'm still alive," he promised. "No matter what weird things you think of doing."

Tears ran down her face as she smiled and carefully put her arms around him. "I didn't think you would want me back after you knew the truth."

"So you planned on telling me at some time?"

"As soon as Jack was behind bars."

Two orderlies opened the curtains to take Nick down for his tests.

"We'll talk about this later," he told her. "Don't marry the man while I'm having an MRI. I might not be able to forgive that."

"Don't be ridiculous. He doesn't want to get married until June."

Sharyn sat in the ladder-back chair for a while after they took Nick away for his tests. What had she done? In telling Nick the truth about her relationship with Jack, she messed up everything she was trying to do. All those awful kisses she'd allowed Jack were wasted if she and Nick got back together. Maybe she could tell Nick she was overcome when she saw him. It would be mostly the truth.

Then she thought about how she felt when Trudy told her Nick was hurt. She wanted to bring Jack down. No question about it. But she wouldn't hurt Nick like that again. He'd almost realized the truth before she told him. Maybe he would be willing to go along with the deception for a while. Like her, he wasn't good with being someone he wasn't, but maybe just this once they could work it out.

With that decision made and not knowing how Nick would feel about it, she left the emergency room and walked downstairs to the morgue. Nick's office and the lab were located in the basement that had once been used as a fallout shelter. It was cold and smelled of mold down there, but it was convenient. If the new sheriff's office was ever finished, there would be a new medical examiner's office located in that building.

Ernie was still in the lab with Ed. He'd sent Marvella home after they'd had a chance to survey the crime scene. He looked up when he saw Sharyn and his heart went out to her. Poor kid couldn't make up her mind. It was obvious she'd been crying. Maybe not to everyone, but he knew her too well to be fooled.

Ed walked up and put his arms around her. "It's gonna be okay. Whoever did this knocked Nick around some, but he's tougher than that."

So much for her thinking no one would notice her red eyes and blotchy face. Red heads didn't cry well. Ignoring it, she hugged Ed back then stepped into her persona as the sheriff. "What can you tell me so far?"

Ernie bagged a piece of broken glass then got to his feet. "The kids got in this morning around ten and found the place like this. Nick was on the floor in his office."

Sharyn looked around at the mess. Books, glass, and metal utensils were thrown everywhere. There was a spot of blood on the floor that made her shiver when she realized it belonged to Nick. "What about Michaelson? Is his body still here?"

"Yeah. Nothing so obvious is missing. Maybe nothing is gone at all," Ernie told her. "It almost looks like a random break-in, except for a few things."

"Like what?"

"Like no one took anything. Nick still has his wallet and wristwatch. His computer is still on his desk."

"Smashed," Ed added. "But still there. A thief wouldn't smash an expensive new computer. He'd take it."

"There was still a bunch of junk food in the kitchen," Ernie continued. "Spare change in a jar. No one broke in here to steal something and surprised Nick while they were doing it. They broke in here to beat Nick up and threw stuff around to make us think otherwise."

"Something personal?" she asked.

"Maybe. I can't say for sure."

Sharyn remembered Jack talking to the man at the party after Nick left last night. Was it possible Jack was sending Nick a warning? If so, was it a warning against pursuing the investigation into Michaelson's death or was it personal?

They wouldn't know until they figured out the puzzle. "I doubt if we will find any fingerprints or DNA to speak of," she observed.

Megan and Keith had been huddled in the corner since she got there. When she heard Sharyn's words, Megan reacted violently. "So you're not even going to bother trying to figure out who did this?" Keith tried to pull her back, but she ignored him and continued, "If you were still dating Nick you'd find some way to catch the person who hurt him. Now it doesn't mean anything to you."

"Easy, young'un," Ernie warned. "You aren't Nick's

only friend here. We've known him a lot longer than you. We'll handle the investigation like we do every other investigation."

Sharyn smiled at Megan. "In fact, this is a good time for you and Keith to show off how much you've learned. Prove me wrong. Find us something here we can work with."

Megan looked up at her and pushed her heavy, black-rimmed glasses back on her face. Her dark eyes were red from crying. "We'll do that, Sheriff. Then you can go out and arrest the bad guys."

"That's how it works." Sharyn nodded. "Call me if you find anything. I don't care how small it is."

"You got it." Keith wanted a part of that action too.

"Nick said something to me about what he'd found examining Michaelson," Sharyn said. "Do either of you know what that is?"

Megan shrugged when she looked at Keith then glanced back at Sharyn. "When did you talk to him? Just now? They said *we* couldn't see him."

Not wanting to make this any worse than it was, Sharyn said, "He called me last night. He wanted to see me today, but he didn't say why."

"He didn't say anything to us," Keith said. "But we could look for his notes and see what we can find."

"Good. Thanks. It could be a few days before Nick is back on his feet. We don't have time to waste if Michaelson's death is a homicide. I'll leave Ed here with you in case whoever did this decides to come back."

"The hospital is posting two security guards for now," Ernie added.

"I'll feel better with one of us here." Sharyn nodded at Ed. "And since you managed to get out of court today, you're my man."

"That's fine," Ed said. "They rescheduled the trial for next month. Maybe we won't be in such a mess by then."

Sharyn glanced at her watch. "I'm sure the county commission would be willing to put off this budget request, but I'm not. We need another person on first shift. If you two can wrap this up, I'm going over to the courthouse."

Ed and Ernie agreed and Sharyn left them there with the two forensic students. She was running late, but if she could catch a few commissioners she could still get them to hear her request.

Joe's injury should make some difference. She hated to use it but she had no choice. Joe was a long way from taking on any kind of position. She could fight for him later. Right now, she needed another warm body at the sheriff's office.

She didn't want to think about the fit Terry was going to pitch when he heard she was splitting up Cari and him. She'd put Cari on days in a heartbeat except that she and Ed had a history. There was a brief romantic relationship that she knew would put Ed in a bad position. She couldn't stand to hear Trudy grind her teeth all day.

The commission meeting was going long. A group of disgruntled citizens was protesting the closing of a road between Diamond Springs and Frog Meadow. Sharyn sat in the front row where the commissioners would see her. She knew they wouldn't end the meeting until they heard what she had to say.

"I've lived on that road all my life," Nate Tucker said. "If you close it, I'll have to maintain it or I won't be able to get out."

Commissioner Betty Fontana shook her head. "Nate, the interstate is practically in your backyard. That's why we're not gonna take care of Tucker Road anymore. You can use the interstate like everyone else."

"That road is the devil's highway. Look at what it's done to our county. We got crime galore and men running around in ladies' underwear on the TV. That's what comes of roads like that. I won't use it."

"Thanks for your input," Commissioner Fontana said as she sat back in her seat. "Anyone else want to speak on this matter?"

Nate banged his fist on the wooden podium. "I'm not done talking."

"Yes you are. Sit down. We'll tell you what we're going to do." Commission chairman Ty Swindoll shook his gavel at the other man.

Without warning, Nate pulled a sawed-off shotgun

out of one leg of his overalls. "This ain't over until I say it's over. Just put that little hammer down, Ty. You're not gonna do anything to my road."

If Sharyn had set it up, she couldn't make a better case for hiring another deputy. Technically, this was Diamond Springs police business. But since she was sitting here and none of the city's finest were at the commission meeting, she supposed she'd handle it. She'd known Nate Tucker and his family all of her life. He wasn't going to shoot anyone. He just wanted to be heard.

Chairman Swindoll put his gavel down and stared at the barrel of the gun. "Put that thing away, Nate. If the TV camera picks up on that you'll go to jail and where will that leave Tilley and your kids?"

"At least they won't have to travel on no interstate," Nate defended. "I'm not putting the gun away."

His eyebrows flew up like blackbirds out of a cornfield when he felt the barrel of Sharyn's Colt in his back and heard her say, "Put it down nice and easy, Nate. Let's not make this any worse than it is already."

Nate put the shotgun on the podium, the business end still pointed toward the commissioners. When he raised his hands, a large sigh of relief filled the meeting room.

Swindoll stood up abruptly and ran from the room toward the restrooms in the hall. Another commissioner got to his feet, but his knees buckled under him and he sank to the floor.

Fontana stood up and put her hands on her hips and

said, "You're in a lot of trouble now, Mr. Tucker. Somebody call a security guard and an officer to help Sheriff Howard with this."

Sharyn let Nate sit down in one of the uncomfortable new chairs purchased recently by the county. He sniffled a little and angrily wiped a tear from his face. "Your daddy wouldn't have let this happen. This is a gross misconduct of justice. I am the wronged party here. Anyone can see that."

"Maybe so." She didn't disagree. "But a shotgun isn't going to solve your problems with the commission."

"Used to solve my problems with those pesky revenuers."

Sharyn almost smiled. Progress didn't catch on as fast outside the city. There were hundreds of people like Nate Tucker in the county. Everyone was lucky it was resolved this easily.

Two security guards and two Diamond Springs police officers escorted Nate from the room, his head hanging low, feet shuffling.

Fontana resumed her seat and took Swindoll's gavel. "Now what do we owe you for that service, Sheriff Howard? I'm assuming you're here about the budget."

Commissioner Harold Lowder still couldn't get to his feet, but he peered over the long table and said, "The budget hearing is over. We can't add anything else right now."

Fontana banged the gavel. "I think maybe we can. I

declare the budget hearing open again. Sheriff Howard, you have the floor."

With three of the five county commissioners shaken but present, Sharyn explained her situation with Joe, asking for a replacement for him and throwing in the part about keeping him on in the office after he went through rehab.

They huddled and argued and finally gave Sharyn most of what she wanted. She had permission to hire someone to take Joe's place and she could have him part-time to begin with in the office.

It was more than she expected. She left the meeting room feeling good about herself. The issue would still have to make it through a public hearing, but by that time everyone in town would know about what happened to Joe. It would be an easy slide.

She walked slowly between the new courthouse annex and the older area that housed the police department and the sheriff's office, checking in with Nick's doctor on her cell phone to see how he was doing.

Outside of a headache and generally feeling like he'd been beaten, Nick was healthy, the doctor said. Too healthy, he hoped, to keep more than overnight. He confided in her that Nick was the worst patient he'd ever had.

Sharyn thanked him and took a deep breath, glad that nothing worse happened. They got away lucky this time. They might not be as fortunate next time.

She kept her own counsel on what she thought happened in the lab. She felt certain the man Jack sent out of the party was the one responsible for what happened to Nick. She could hear Ernie asking what her proof was, besides gut instinct, the way he did when she first started the job after her father was killed.

She would give almost anything to talk to Ernie now, to really feel like there wasn't anything she couldn't say to him. But she couldn't take any chances on giving herself away, especially now when she might have Jack for Michaelson's death and trying to tamper with the evidence Nick was looking into.

It was a warning. She had no doubt of that. It said, *don't look any further or it could get worse.* She was sick of warnings, tired of secrets. She wanted to know once and for all, out in the daylight. She wanted to see the headlines in the *Diamond Springs Gazette* proclaiming that everyone knew the terrible things Jack had done.

Of course, Selma and Nick seemed to think it was obvious that she was dating Jack to expose him. She was surprised Jack wanted to marry her. Was it only because Selma and Nick knew her so well? Or did Jack suspect but let it go because it played into his plans to beat Selma for the senate race?

"Earth to Sheriff Howard." Ernie passed her going into the office. "You've been standing there since I pulled up. Is everything okay?"

"Everything's fine. I got permission to hire another deputy. I even got money for Joe part-time." She told him about Nate Tucker and he laughed.

"That boy is lucky he can tell his head from a turnip. I wouldn't call that much of a rescue. The commissioners were more likely to choke themselves on their own rhetoric than Nate was to be able to shoot any of them." Ernie was still chuckling as they went downstairs into the office.

The awful smell of disinfectant and basement mildew with steam heat going full blast hit them as they opened the door. Sharyn took off her hat and hung it on the wall. "We have to get out of here."

"Could've been worse." Ernie sniffed, fingering his mustache. "Could've been an old barn that smelled like manure."

Trudy handed Sharyn her messages. "You're full of good thoughts today, aren't you?"

"You bet. I think Annie and I have decided to secretly elope. We can be in Las Vegas at one of those swanky hotels and you all can watch the whole thing on the Internet. How's that for technology?"

"Sounds interesting." Sharyn poured herself a cup of coffee into a chicken-shaped mug. "Why the hurry?"

"I'm the same age as Joe. I'm not in any danger of being called to the Middle East and losing my leg, but we've put this off for a good while and neither one of us is getting any younger. I'd like a few years of wedded bliss before I die."

"Then I think you should go for it. Just because the first try was a little choppy doesn't mean the next one won't be okay."

He laughed. "Thanks. I think you must be the mistress of understatement. I blew the whole thing last time by spending a few minutes alone at the computer with Cari. *That* sure won't happen again."

"Did I hear someone mention my name?" Cari stepped out of the boiler room/conference area. She smiled at them and tossed her shoulder-length blond hair.

Trudy shrugged when Sharyn's eyes narrowed on her. "Nobody asked me if anyone else was here. You two should keep that kind of talk private."

Cari glanced between the three of them, truly not certain what they'd been talking about. When no one appeared to be forthcoming on what was happening, she shrugged and started talking about what she found on Michaelson's computer. "It was as clean as anything could be. I looked at it in every direction I could think of. If he had something on that hard drive, someone must've wiped it."

"Have you tried one of the Homeland Security Recovery programs?" Terry asked as he came in and hung up his coat.

Cari glanced at him like she would a fly on the wall. "I used Norton on it. Nothing showed up."

"You didn't give it long enough. If I wiped all the information off a computer, you wouldn't find it in a couple of hours."

She stared at him, blue eyes wide, her hands on her slender hips. "I didn't realize you knew something about computers."

Terry folded his arms across his wide chest. "I'd be glad to give you a hand with that."

"All right. Maybe between the two of us we can figure it out."

Sharyn asked both of them what they were doing there so early. "You've got about eight hours before you're due in."

"Too much happening, Sheriff," Terry said. "How can someone sleep when it's important to find out what's going on?"

Cari nodded. "That's why I'm here too."

"All right," Sharyn replied. "Just don't let me find you sleeping when you're supposed to be working."

"Excuse me, Sheriff," Cari said. "But you're the last person in the world to lecture someone about working double shifts. If I had a dollar for every time Ernie told you to go home, I'd be sipping drinks with little umbrellas in them on a beach in the Caribbean."

Ernie, showing no remorse at his earlier remarks

about Cari, agreed with her. "Sorry, Sheriff. She's got you there."

Sharyn sat down at her desk. "Are you two going to find things on that computer or what?"

Terry winked at Sharyn as he followed Cari into the conference room. There was apparently more than one way to get noticed.

Trudy answered the phone and told Sharyn it was for her. It was Nick's doctor. "Sheriff, I need you to come over here before I kill him. He says he has something that can't wait. Something about a murder you're investigating."

"Why don't you put him on the phone?" She didn't know if she was up to seeing Nick again today. One session of tears was about all she could handle in a day.

"He won't do that. He wants you to come over here."

"All right. We'll be right over." She put down the phone and turned to Ernie. "Let's take a walk down to the hospital. Nick told me last night he had something about Michaelson. Apparently he won't behave until he tells us."

Ernie scratched his head. "Why didn't he tell you when you were up there earlier?"

"Let's not go into that." She put on her jacket and hat, picked up her gun and cell phone. "Trudy, you keep the computer nerds in check. We'll be back as soon as we can."

Ernie and Sharyn walked back through the courthouse annex and came out on Main Street. The wind whistled along the sidewalk, but the sun was warm on their heads.

"This was a warning." Ernie echoed Sharyn's earlier thoughts. "Somebody doesn't want us snooping into Michaelson's death."

"You're right. Although we can't know for sure it's all about Michaelson. Maybe it's about the girl."

"Maybe." Ernie stared up at the blue sky while they waited for the light to change. "But we all know Michaelson didn't get that house being a junior partner at Percy's law firm. I pulled his bank records this morning. The man was packing it in. Either he was embezzling or he was making plenty of money at a part-time job."

"We should talk to Mr. Percy on our way back from the hospital. Maybe he can shed some light on Michaelson's fortune."

Nick's room was on the third floor. Ernie and Sharyn took the elevator up and weren't surprised to find nurses already ignoring his demands for attention. One nurse cautioned them about visiting him when they asked for his room number.

Ernie chuckled as they followed the hall to Nick's room. "The man has only been here a little while and they already hate him. Good thing he isn't technically a member of the sheriff's department. We have a reputation to uphold when they bring us in here."

"And what would that be?" Sharyn asked him before she opened the door.

"We're always polite no matter how much pain we're in. We never complain and never harass the nurses." He sniffed and removed his hat. "That's who we are."

"I try to get out as soon as I can." She pushed open the door. "That's who *I* am."

The sun was shining through the window with a view of Diamond Lake. Nick was sitting up in bed, typing something on his laptop. He looked up when they came in and took off his glasses. "Sorry. I was expecting a nurse."

Ernie glanced out of the window. "I wouldn't expect one if I were you. They have your face on a dart board down there at the nurses' station. Nice view."

Sharyn took off her hat, feeling awkward after telling Nick the truth. *Now what? Anything I say is going to sound stupid. I can't believe I told him everything. He wasn't dying.* "How are you feeling?"

"Like somebody sneaked in the lab behind me, hit me in the head, and beat me up. Not great."

"You said you had something important to tell me about Michaelson last night." She fell back on being the sheriff. "Would you like to talk about that now?"

He stared at her. "Am I being interrogated, Sheriff? Do I need my lawyer?"

"Why do you always have to make everything so

hard? Is there *anything* you can do without giving someone a bad time?"

Ernie stepped away from the window. "Can you two please knock it off?" He glared at them. "The question is legitimate, Nick. Answer it."

"Yes, sir." Nick saluted him smartly then groaned as it hurt his injured arm. "I have some information about Michaelson that you aren't going to like." He smiled at Sharyn. "Or maybe you will."

"Just tell us," she encouraged, trying not to lose her temper. Nick always had such a flair for the dramatic.

"Michaelson had carbon monoxide in his lungs. Right now, I would rule him a suicide."

Chapter Nine

"**N**o way!" Sharyn said. "There has to be more to it!"

"I'm sorry. I wish there was. But unless I find something else that makes me think different, it looks like Michaelson killed himself. Maybe the girl was involved."

Ernie leaned his fists on the end of the bed. "That's the best you can do? You dragged us over here to tell us there's nothing to investigate?"

"I thought you'd appreciate knowing what I found before you go through all the trouble of investigating the death as a homicide." Nick shrugged then grimaced. "That's all I got to before I was hit in the head. I suppose everything is gone."

"No," Sharyn replied. "Everything is a mess, but

Michaelson was still on the table where you left him. I was surprised too."

"Why bother doing all this if you aren't planning on disrupting the investigation?" He looked at Sharyn and Ernie.

"Did you get anything before you were assaulted?" she asked him. "A smell. A sound. Anything?"

He closed his eyes and searched his memory. "Nothing. Sorry. I was intent on Michaelson. Whoever it was took me totally by surprise."

Ernie shook his head. "It's pretty strange. Sharyn and I agree it was some kind of warning. But if Michaelson is a suicide, why bother? And if not, why not take the evidence? I can think of plenty of places in the mountains where no one would ever find him."

"That's just the thing," Sharyn said. "He was set up for us to find in the first place. Why bother taking something someone wanted us to see?"

"I'd like to know why someone bothered hitting me if I was doing what they wanted me to do." Nick leaned his head back against the pillow, his face strained.

The head nurse bustled into the room and told them they would have to leave. "Dr. Thomopolis needs his rest or there's no point in him being here."

"Sounds good to me." Nick started to throw off the sheet that covered him.

The nurse, all five feet, ninety pounds of her,

dropped into a karate stance. "You just tuck that sheet back in! I'm working on my brown belt and I've been looking for a sparring partner all day."

Nick put the sheet back. "This place gets worse every time I come upstairs. The morgue is better. At least it's quiet."

Sharyn smiled. "And messy right now. Just the way you like it."

Ernie walked out of the room, but Nick caught Sharyn's hand as she turned to go. "We have to talk. Can you come back later?"

"I'll try."

"Try hard."

The nurse put the plastic sleeve on the thermometer. "Visiting hours are six to nine. Don't come back before that."

Sharyn squeezed Nick's hand. "I'll be back." She closed the door behind her as she joined Ernie. "None of that made much sense."

"I know. Let's check downstairs before we go. See if the kids have managed to put anything together yet."

Megan and Keith were slowly sifting through the rubble that was left in Nick's office and the lab. Ernie asked them if they could tell if anything was missing.

"Not yet." Megan tossed a piece of shattered coffee cup into a plastic bag. "We need a little time, Deputy. We're not miracle workers."

"It's not something obvious," Keith answered. "If

anything was taken, it wasn't anything important. Dr. Thomopolis' notes, the victim's charts. Everything looks like it's just the way it was when we went home yesterday. Except messed up."

"We won't bother you again," Sharyn promised. "We were upstairs talking to Nick and thought we'd stop by."

"How is he?" Keith asked.

"He's gonna live," Ernie told him. "He might not be doing any figure skating for a while, but he's got a hard head. He'll be fine."

Megan frowned at him. "Figure skating? Does Nick skate?"

Ernie rolled his eyes. "Never mind. Call us if you find anything."

"I want to check something before we go." Sharyn headed for the morgue.

Ernie followed her. "What are you looking for?"

"I'm not sure." She opened the drawer with the hit-and-run victim's body. It opened smoothly without a sound. She stared into the empty space where the girl should be. "What about that?"

"That's weird." He scratched his head. "Maybe she's somewhere else."

Megan and Keith came into the room and the four of them looked everywhere, but Michelle's body was gone.

"That doesn't make much sense," Keith said. "Why would anyone want *her* body?"

"We were all so intent on Michaelson," Sharyn offered. "The girl was more important."

"But we found Nick's notes," Megan argued. "Michaelson was a suicide. He killed the girl then killed himself. Case closed. Why take her body?"

"I think that's what we have to figure out." Sharyn closed the long drawer. "Keep in touch."

With the new circumstances in mind, Sharyn and Ernie went to talk with District Attorney Eldeon Percy. He was in his signature pose, head resting on one hand, eyes closed. He listened as Sharyn told him what happened. His crisp, white linen suit was spotlessly clean as always. He was never seen wearing anything else.

When she finished speaking, he opened his eyes and nodded. "I don't hear a request for my help in this matter so I assume you've come to ask me about Alan."

"We were a little confused by his lifestyle. Was he making enough money working for your firm to have a house like that?" Sharyn sat across the wide, oak desk from him.

"Having not seen the house, it would be difficult for me to answer that question," the DA evaded.

"We took some pictures." Ernie spread them on his desk. "I also checked his bank account this morning. As you can see, Mr. Michaelson made some very large deposits in the last year."

Percy looked carefully at the pictures. "Not being a

real estate broker, I'm afraid I don't know much about house values. This looks like a very nice house, but to give my opinion on whether or not Alan could afford this house is out of my expertise."

Eldeon was always careful. Sharyn knew not to expect too much unless she asked the right questions. He'd been a lawyer for too long to get tangled in anything that might lead down the wrong path.

"What about the cash deposits to his account?" Ernie asked.

"Again, Deputy, I would like to help you. But outside of telling you that this is a great deal more than Alan made from his salary with my ex-law firm, I can't answer you."

Ernie sat back, exasperated. "Is there *anything* helpful you can tell us, Mr. Percy?"

The DA smiled in a slippery way. "That you shouldn't be wasting your time here with me?"

Sharyn got to her feet. "Thank you for your time, Mr. Percy." She waited while Ernie shook hands with the district attorney before she added, "One more thing, sir."

Percy lifted one brow. "Yes, Sheriff?"

"I'd like to get a look at all the cases Mr. Michaelson was working on. Could you arrange that for me?"

"You know that information is protected by the Constitution."

"I don't need to see any of the pertinent data, sir. I'd

just like to know what was on his desk. I'm sure I don't have to tell you that a search warrant would be valid in this case."

The DA nodded. "I'll see the information gets to your desk, Sheriff. Please let me know if you need anything else."

Ernie nudged Sharyn with his elbow as they walked out of the DA's office. "What was that all about? Without anything to go with it, what difference does it make what cases Michaelson was working on?"

She smiled an imitation of Percy's smile. "We have his laptop. Any information we find there is ours. If we know what cases that information goes with, we might have something that will help us."

"Slick." Ernie nodded in appreciation of her tactics. "You're one smart cookie."

When they got back to the office, Trudy had ordered lunch for everyone, pizza from the new delivery store a couple of blocks away. Terry and Cari could barely wait for them to take off their coats, their eyes dancing with excitement over what they'd found on Michaelson's laptop.

Ed had left the investigation at the hospital to their security when he was called out on a storm-related emergency. The four of them still in the office sat around Sharyn's desk to talk about what they'd learned.

After taking a bite of cheese pizza, Terry was finally able to explain what they'd found. "Everything. The mother lode. Big deals. Small deals. Michaelson must have been like the secretary for the big bubba club around here."

"He implicates almost every person in the city and county government," Cari said. "Judges. Commissioners. Councilmen."

"Senators?" Sharyn glanced up at her.

"Yes." Cari's blue eyes shone with victory. "Someone could write a book with all the information about Caison Talbot and Jack Winter."

Sharyn tried not to get too excited when she heard what they had to say. It might be something they could use. It might be a waste of time if it couldn't be corroborated. If Michaelson had one thing Jack did on a night his alibi was perfect, a judge would throw the rest of the information away. "We have to move very quietly and thoroughly on this. Let's make a backup of the information. Then we'll give a copy to the DA's office."

"Are you sure that's a good idea?" Trudy asked from her desk. "Things have a way of disappearing around here."

"That's why we're only giving them a copy." Sharyn turned to Cari. "Did Michaelson mention anything about Eldeon Percy?"

"Not a word," Terry said.

"He didn't mention Toby either," Cari added about her ADA boyfriend.

"That's good, right?" Ernie asked. "Did Michaelson mention anyone on the job?"

"Only David." Terry shook his head. "I'm afraid his death happened because he was dirty."

"He mentions your father, Sheriff," Cari said quietly. "You should read everything before you release it. There may be some things you want to delete."

Sharyn wasn't able to tell them that both David and her father were working with the FBI. It was hard to let them think her father had taken money from Jack or anyone else, but until this was resolved, she had to let them think whatever they wanted. "No special treatment. If a name is in that computer, we'll have to check it out."

After finishing lunch, Cari and Terry made several copies of the information on Michaelson's laptop. Sharyn dispatched them to give two of the copies to Mr. Percy and Toby Fisher. Terry was unhappy when Cari designated him to take his copy to the DA while she took hers to her boyfriend.

Trudy consoled him with a hug and told him that Rome wasn't built in a day. "You work with her. Use your time wisely."

"Is that what happened with you and Ed?" Terry asked.

"He swept me off my feet." Trudy blushed as she spoke. "He's the best thing that ever happened to me."

"And that's the best abbreviated version I've heard," Ernie muttered to Sharyn as they put one copy of Michaelson's data in their safe.

"They're happy together," Sharyn pointed out. "What's your problem?"

"You know Ed didn't deserve Trudy."

"Would it have been better for Trudy to be alone the rest of her life?"

He shook his head. "Good point. Now, what do we do with the laptop?"

"We keep it here locked up in the evidence room. I take a copy and you take a copy since Cari didn't find you on Michaelson's list."

"What are you talking about? Did you think I'd be on that list?"

Sharyn leaned her hands on the table between them. "Someone, maybe not someone in this computer, has been giving Jack information for years, at least since I became sheriff. Maybe before."

"And you thought it was me?"

She shrugged and sat down with the laptop in front of her. "I don't know who it is."

"Well I'll be."

She opened up the laptop and turned it on. "I'm going to read through this whole thing. I want you to do the same later. Something could happen that we'll lose this information no matter how careful we are."

"Okay. I guess I'm going out on patrol. I'll read it later. Be sure to call me if you find my name in there."

"I didn't want to think you were involved with Jack, Ernie. I've tried to keep an open mind."

"Open mind?" he erupted. "I've known you since you were a baby. How could you think I would betray you or your daddy that way?"

Sharyn could see he was quivering with rage. He was hurt too. She wasn't sure what to say to him, but she knew she had to try. "I found a journal when we moved out of the old station. It was in code. I didn't tell you because you've always acted like there were things I shouldn't know about my father."

Ernie ran a finger across his mustache. "Sharyn, I haven't been totally honest with you. I know why your daddy's name is in the computer."

"I do too. He was working with the FBI. So was David. Dad kept that journal to try and implicate everyone he found working with the good-old-boy network. They probably found out what he was doing and had him killed."

"I can't believe it." He sat down abruptly like his legs wouldn't hold him any longer. "I *knew* something was wrong. Maybe your daddy wasn't sure about me either."

Sharyn touched his hand. They were on the verge of destroying Jack without her plan. She was going to tell Ernie the truth. "Or maybe he was trying to keep you alive." She told him the journal was stolen almost right after she started decoding it. "I agreed to go to work with Agent Brewster after David's funeral. We both believed I could appeal to Jack's emotional side. He's always been pretty clear that he was interested in me."

"I don't want you to take this the wrong way." He gripped her hand. "But I think Jack is after you because you favor Selma so much. I think he was trying to get what he couldn't have."

"Oh great! And here I was thinking I was like some kind of southern Mata Hari!"

"As long as you're not taking yourself too seriously." He looked at her grandmother's ring on her slender finger. "I don't know if he's serious about you or using you to get around Selma's bid for the Senate."

"I think he wanted me before that," she replied tartly. "I know I'm not a beauty queen, Ernie. But I'm not *that* bad."

"You're a beautiful woman. I didn't mean that. I meant that I can't believe he thinks you really want to be with him. Not even with *his* ego. So I have to assume he realizes what you're doing and is taking advantage of it. Don't underestimate him."

"I try not to." She looked at the laptop screen. Michaelson had wallpaper of a robot lifting the earth. "I think Nick was assaulted because he and Jack got into it at the fundraiser. I know Jack doesn't like people who stand up to him."

"Except for you."

"I think he thinks it's cute when I argue with him."

"That could be his downfall."

"The thing I'm wondering about is this whole sequence of events. Let's say Michaelson is dating Michelle. Something happens and he decides to run her down. He drives back home and closes the garage door with the engine running. He dies in his Hummer for us to find."

"Suicide, like Nick said."

"Except for the doors to the house being left open and the power being off at the gate when Terry and I pulled up. We thought all the power was off, but everything was on at the house."

"So you're still stuck on Jack having a hand in this? Where's your proof? If you're thinking this is something Jack did because of the information on the laptop, why didn't he take it with him?"

"I don't know," she admitted. "But the timing, Jack coming in as this happened, the information on the laptop that could send him away for the rest of his life, is too good."

"You think Michaelson was trying to get something from Jack because he had all this information?"

"That would be one reason for Jack to kill him. But he's more thorough than that. He would've taken what he needed from the house."

"That doesn't make any sense." Ernie shifted in his chair. "Jack killing Michaelson for this information, I can see that. Even finding someway to do it that makes it look like a suicide. But there's no way he left the laptop for us to find. That shoots your whole theory."

"Maybe he was in town but he didn't kill Michaelson himself. I'm sure he sent someone after Nick at the fundraiser. If that's the case, maybe his hired hand screwed up. Maybe he left the laptop behind."

"And maybe he thought Nick had it." Ernie's eyes gleamed. "Maybe that's what they were after at the lab."

"Which would make sense if someone hadn't taken Michelle's body. I don't get it."

He got up from his chair and stood for a moment staring at the table. "We'll have to figure it out. With this information, we might be able to put a lot of our problems behind us. Maybe I could retire."

She laughed. "Maybe *I* could retire. I've had the toughest job. I had to kiss Jack Winter."

"I think that sounds like a personal choice. I'm going out on patrol. Let me know if you find anything else. And find some time to go and see Joe. He feels bad enough about all of this. Let him know you still care about him. It would mean a lot."

Sharyn agreed to find time in her schedule to go and see Joe. It would have to be before or after she went to see Nick. Somewhere in between there, she would probably be talking with Jack. She could only hope at this point that Michaelson's information was correct and nothing about the new investigation would get back to him. He might not be willing to overlook his fiancée trying to put him in prison.

She sat at the desk for an hour after Ernie left, reading through the files on the laptop. Michaelson was thorough in naming the event that happened, when it happened and who was responsible from the person who did the job to the person who hired him. Going through the data was like a who's who of people from all over the state.

It broke her heart to read some of the names. They were people she knew and trusted. Many of them weren't real players in the sense that they were involved in illegal activities that ranged from gambling to drugs and prostitution. They were people who did favors for return favors from political figures.

She wasn't sure how to handle some of the information. Caison figured prominently in the text. Her mother would be devastated. Maybe he could make a deal and testify for the state. Other people she recognized wouldn't truly be considered as doing illegal deeds. They might not even be mentioned.

Jack would be going away for a long time if she could find corroboration on some of the information. One big event documented in the computer was Trudy's first husband's death. Jack had Ben killed after he had some horses taken away from Jack and accused him of cruelty. Chavis Whitley, a small-time criminal who was later arrested for another crime, did the deed. Fortunately for Chavis, Ernie killed him when he tried to escape. At least when that information came out, Trudy wouldn't feel the need to go after the man herself.

Sharyn realized it could take years to go through all of the events Michaelson documented. She needed only one to make a case against Jack, but it would have to be one she could make stick. After that, the rest would have to be investigated, but Jack would be behind bars as it happened.

There was one entry that she puzzled over. It wasn't spelled out like the others. It concerned the sheriff's department. She knew it could be her mole. It was like Michaelson purposely didn't say exactly who was involved. The entry listed several times that the mole gave them information about cases. All the dates were since she became sheriff. Nothing from when her father was alive.

She was fairly sure it was David passing information. It might have been how he first got involved with Jack.

Sharyn talked to Nick about it when she went to visit him at 6:30 that evening. "Between David, Jack, and Michaelson in the DA's office, it was like living in a fishbowl. They knew everything."

"Let's go back to you looking up Ernie's name on the laptop." Nick sat up straighter in the chair the nurses let him occupy. He was going home in the morning and they were sick of arguing with him. "Did you look up *my* name?"

"I went through *all* the information. I was looking for my father's name. You and Ernie came next."

"How does Ernie feel about that? Or am I the only one who knows he was a suspect?"

"I told Ernie. I think he understood."

"I guess that means I understand too." He closed his eyes. "But you're straining my limits of understanding, Sharyn. I think I can handle you thinking I might be ratting you out to Jack, but I don't think I can handle that *and* you marrying him."

"I don't plan to marry him. With this information and a little leg work, I shouldn't have to pretend to be with him anymore. This is what we've looked for since my father died. We have Jack and everyone else who ever took money from the good-old-boys network."

"Including Caison and a half dozen other well known figures in town," he reminded her.

"I can't help that. I'm going to give Caison an opportunity to turn state's evidence against Jack and everyone else. We'll see how it goes."

"Okay. Where are *we* with everything else?"

"I think Jack or someone working for him broke into your office and assaulted you because he thought you had the laptop. The only thing I don't understand is why they took Michelle's body."

Nick smiled. "That's interesting. But I was talking about 'us' everything else."

"Oh, sorry." She felt her face get hot. Red heads also blushed more than anyone else. "I don't really know what to say. I'm sorry I felt like I had to do this. If I'd known Michaelson was going to die and leave us these answers, I wouldn't have let Jack near me. You know that. I thought I was doing the right thing. I didn't want you to be involved in case something went wrong."

"That was very thoughtful of you. I appreciate that it was hard for you to do." He stared at her then looked away. "But I'm having a hard time accepting that you were willing to trade our relationship to put someone in jail."

"It's not someone. It's Jack. He killed my father and ruined hundreds of people's lives. He had Ben and David killed."

"I know. And I think I'll get over this. But right now, I'm having a hard time. I love you, Sharyn. But I don't know what kind of future we have together. How will I ever know when a case you're working on becomes so important that you're willing to forget about me?"

"I didn't expect you to understand. I knew when I broke up with you it might be over for good. That was a chance I had to take."

"I hope that makes you feel better because it doesn't do a thing for me."

She got slowly to her feet. "I think I should go now.

Get some rest. We still have some work to do trying to figure out what happened with Michaelson."

He looked up at her. "Is that it? We can always fall back on our professional relationship? You're a good sheriff, but you have a lot to learn about trusting people who love you."

Sharyn didn't know what to say. She accepted the criticism and left him. She wandered out of the hospital without seeing anything around her. It wasn't that she ever expected to get Nick back again. She told herself from the moment she thought of her plan that she would be sacrificing her heart to put Jack away for good.

It seemed like it might be okay between her and Nick when they talked after he'd been injured. For a while her heart wasn't so heavy. She thought he might be able to understand and forgive her.

Now she knew it was over. It was the brief time she wasn't sure that pained her, she told herself as she shivered in the cold air standing outside the hospital. Tomorrow she would go back to work and everything would be fine. She lost Nick for nothing since she found Michaelson's information. But she was going to win the war against the corruption that had hurt so many people in Diamond Springs.

She shook her head, told herself to focus, and walked back to the parking deck to get her Jeep. She had one more stop. She hoped it wasn't too late to see Joe. After that, she could go home and try to put it all behind her.

Diamond Springs was quiet around her after the rush of people getting home from work and settling in for the night. The cold air enhanced the lights around the lake in the center of town as she drove toward Joe's house.

She felt like she was carved of wood, stiff and un-yielding. Maybe that's the way she really was. Nick said as much and maybe he was right. She was willing to sac-rifice the most important person in her life for her job. If things had been different and she'd become a lawyer as she planned instead of taking her father's place when he was killed, would she have gone after the goal as hard?

Sarah welcomed Sharyn when she knocked on the door. The house was warm and smelled of apple pie and cinnamon. There was a fire in the hearth behind Joe where he sat playing with his daughters and their new puppy. "Sit down and I'll get you a piece of pie and some coffee." Sarah hugged her. "It must be cold out there. You're freezing. Come in and get warm."

Sharyn sat in the chair. Joe looked up at her and smiled. "Hey there. Sorry I can't jump right back into work. I'm not doing much jumping at all right now. Are you guys doing okay?"

The girls were laughing and the puppy was barking. Sharyn looked at the bandaged stump of Joe's leg. She couldn't believe he was sitting there thinking about the job. What was wrong with all of them? He should be happy to be home and alive, not worrying about getting back to work.

"Sharyn?" He got her attention after several tries. "Is something wrong?"

She wasn't sure how it happened, but she ended up sitting on the floor beside him. She was crying and the girls and the puppy were gone. She told him everything that had happened while he was away. He put his arms around her and they watched the flames in the fireplace for a long time.

"You know, you were always a stubborn little girl. Always serious and too smart for your own good. You let Uncle Joe tell you a thing or two now. I can handle this thing with my leg. I could handle them sending me into that awful place. But it's only because I know I have Sarah and the girls to come home to. They keep me going. Sarah has always been there for me, even when we had bad times."

He looked into her eyes. "You and Nick should work this out. You shouldn't be so serious. You have to let some things go or you'll never last in this business. Don't *ever* put your job before the people you love again. Your daddy wouldn't have done that and he wouldn't have wanted you to do it for him."

"I think it's too late for me and Nick. I don't know what I was thinking. But I am where I put myself. No one made me do this."

Joe shook his head. "There's no such thing. Nick loves you. You love him. You remember that time me and Sarah split up for a few weeks? I knew it was my fault. I found a way to get her to take me back. You can do the same thing."

"How?" She wiped a tear from her eye. "I don't know what else to do."

"You're smart. You'll think of something. You always do."

Chapter Ten

Sharyn spent a restless night thinking about what she could do to win Nick back. She was up at 3 A.M. searching the Internet through Ten Ways To Get Your Man Back and other similar websites. By five, she was so full of ridiculous suggestions she would never do, that she showered, dressed, and went into the office. Nick was right. She always fell back on her work.

Cari and Terry were filling out paperwork when she got there. They didn't mention anything about her working too many hours. They looked at her and knew better.

"Quiet night?" she asked them.

"Not too bad," Cari said. "Ernie said you're hiring

174

someone new for the nightshift. Is that to take my place or Terry's?"

"Terry's. We need someone on dayshift to replace Joe. Ed needs a partner." Sharyn hoped she wouldn't make her go into detail on why that had to be Terry.

Cari nodded. "I see."

"I don't," Terry replied. "I was just getting used to this and making some progress. I think you should hire someone for the dayshift. Cari and I are getting along fine."

For making progress, put making progress with Cari, Sharyn understood. But Ed needed a partner and they didn't need another office romance. "Ed likes the idea of working with you, Terry. It won't be easy for him to break in a new partner after so many years working with Joe. I need you on dayshift."

Sharyn didn't want to lose him. He was a good deputy, but his attachment to Cari when she was almost engaged to Toby Fisher was probably another good reason for him not to work with her.

"I see." Terry frowned. "Maybe after we break in the new guy, I could transfer back to nights."

"I can't promise anything." Sharyn turned on her computer. "But we'll see."

Terry seemed to be satisfied with that and Cari didn't complain about breaking in a new partner. Maybe it was better for her too. She had to be aware of Terry's feelings for her.

With that behind her, Sharyn started in on trying to prove one of the incidents in Michaelson's journal was real.

Trudy came in at seven and said good morning. Seeing her, remembering her terrible grief after Ben's death, Sharyn wished she could do something with what happened to him. But with Chavis dead, there would be no one left to corroborate Jack's involvement in what happened.

Ernie and Ed came in and went back out to help with an accident on the Interstate. They also took a call about a dog in Bell's Creek that was reportedly running loose and threatening children on the streets. They arranged to meet animal control out there in case they needed assistance.

Agent Brewster called Sharyn's cell phone and told her his team was working at Michaelson's house. He promised to keep her up to date with whatever they found. She told him about what they found on the laptop and arranged to get a copy to him. Maybe he would have better luck finding something they could prove against Jack.

She was closing her cell phone when something on the computer caught her eye. It was Michaelson's account of how Jack had ruined Jill Madison-Farmer's life. It was told in such a clinical, detached way that it was hard to believe it was real.

Jack had hired two men. She recognized their names.

They planted evidence the police would find and were responsible for her supposed drug habit, injecting her with heroine then tipping the drug squad about her.

Sharyn tapped her fingers on the laptop as she gazed sightlessly across the room. *Could it be this easy?* If the two men could be found and persuaded to testify against Jack, she'd have him. Both men were two-time losers who'd been in trouble all of their lives. Would she be able to convince them it would be worth their while to take Jack down?

She'd known, just as Jill had, that Jack was responsible for her downfall. Jill was investigating the death of an inmate who'd called Sharyn with information about her father's death. Before she could get there to question him, he was found dead in his cell at State Prison in Raleigh. His partner was injured but still alive. Not surprisingly, he decided to keep his mouth shut.

Jill went after Jack's dark side with a vengeance. For a while, he ignored her. Then Sharyn got a phone call about Jill being picked up on the street. She was arrested for using drugs and being a dealer. She was tried and convicted despite Sharyn's best efforts. Jill lost her license to practice law and soon after, lost her husband and children. Not a day went by that Sharyn didn't feel guilty about being part of her downfall.

But maybe she could make it right. Jill's life would never be the same as it was, but everyone would know the truth. She could hold her head up again.

Sharyn's cell phone rang and she answered it without thinking.

"What are you up to, angel?"

Jack's voice made her jump. She closed her laptop even though she knew he wasn't in the room with her. That was how he made her feel. Bringing him to justice would be a unique pleasure. "Hello. I'm reading some files."

"Do they have anything to do with the FBI investigating Michaelson's death?"

"Not really," she lied. "Why?"

"I thought we had an understanding. I thought you understood that I don't want Michaelson's death investigated."

"Is there some reason for that, Jack?"

"Isn't it enough that I'm asking you not to get involved?"

"I'm not. Agent Brewster pushed his way in on this. I don't understand the FBI's involvement, but they usually don't ask my opinion."

His voice sounded a little irritated as he continued. "Find some way to call him off. I have good reasons for this."

"Do you have something to hide?"

He laughed. "Do *you* have something to hide?"

"Not really."

"Of course you do. We all do. As the keeper of many

secrets in this county, Sharyn, I'm telling you to get the FBI out of this."

She almost hung up on him. Who did he think he was, asking her to impede an FBI investigation? Even if she wasn't the instigator of the search, she wouldn't have done what he asked. "I think you've forgotten who I am."

"The same person your father was before he died?"

Sharyn caught her breath at his veiled threat. "I'll do what I can. You'll have to share some of those secrets with me one day, Jack."

"Good girl. I'll be glad to share everything with you as my wife. Do you have that answer for me yet? How angry can you be that I've asked you to spend the rest of your life with me?"

"You have to know it wasn't the asking. It was the way you *assumed* I would say yes." She played with a pencil on her desk. "I'll let you know when I have an answer."

"Don't leave me hanging too long, darling."

The phone went dead in her hand. She closed it, picked up her gun and jacket. "I'm going out, Trudy. Call me if you need me."

"Where will you be?" Trudy turned back to her as she finished handling a complaint from a man who was objecting to a new stop sign at the end of his road.

"I'm going out to interview a couple of suspects. I'll be back later."

The phone rang again and Trudy's brow lifted. "You know you shouldn't be going out alone. Call someone for backup. I know you're the big bad sheriff, but that won't save you from getting hurt. I shouldn't have to tell you that."

Sharyn smiled. "Better answer that. I'll be in touch."

She walked out to her Jeep pondering Trudy's words. She knew she was right. She was going to have to impress both men responsible for what happened to Jill with a fear of the law like they had never known before if she was going to get them to turn on Jack. Both men were experienced in dealing with police. They would smell blood if she went in alone. She knew her badge wouldn't protect her.

The problem was there were only a few people she felt certain she could trust. Nick was still incapacitated. Ernie was out taking care of business with Ed. Joe was hurt.

That left the second and third-shift deputies. They were already working extra hours. She didn't want to call them in unless she had to. They had work to do and she depended on them carrying their shifts.

The door to the basement opened and the answer to her problem walked through it. Jefferson Two-Rivers, Sam's brother and the sheriff of Cherokee County, took off his hat and nodded to Sharyn. "Morning, Sheriff. I came by to pick up that prisoner you caught for me. I almost put it off until the roads got better then I heard there was another storm on the way."

She stared at him wondering how he would react to her request for help. She knew she could trust him. They'd worked together before.

He held out the necessary paperwork for the transfer then realized she hadn't spoken. "Is something wrong? Is there some reason you're staring at me like I'm Santa?"

She laughed. "Not Santa. Maybe Dirty Harry."

"Dirty who?"

"I'll fill you in. Trudy will take care of the paperwork." She handed the documents to her assistant. "We'll be back later."

"Later? Now it's the two of you going some place I'm not supposed to know about? I think you should call Ernie before you go." Trudy rambled on. "I don't want to be responsible for something bad happening."

Jefferson rubbed his hands together. "This is sounding better by the minute. I don't know who Dirty Harry is, but it sounds like fun to me."

Sharyn didn't say anything else to Trudy as she put on her jacket and walked out the door with Jefferson behind her. Trudy tried to call Ernie and Ed, but got no response. "Just how important is some dog out in the county compared to the sheriff's life?"

Sharyn explained the situation to Jefferson. He didn't ask any questions. "You know I'm there whatever you need to do."

She glanced at him as they climbed in her Jeep. His

dark eyes were shadowed by the wide brim of his Stetson. His high cheek bones and solid nose made his face strong and as dependable as she knew he was. "Thanks. You know I'd do the same for you."

He smiled. "I know. That's why I'm here."

Sharyn drove out to the newly renovated Stag Inn Doe, hoping to find Marti Martin still working there. He'd worked on and off all over the county since she became sheriff. None of the jobs lasted too long and most of them involved something illegal.

He had been hired to work at the Stag Inn Doe by legendary stock car driver Duke Beatty, who was later killed in strange circumstances. Sharyn later learned that Duke was working with Jack. She couldn't prove it at the time and Duke's death kept her from pursuing it. But Marti was mentioned as one of the men who helped Jack get Jill out of the picture.

Barker Rosemont owned the establishment now. The building had been originally owned by his father who'd lost it in a card game. It was on the county line which made jurisdiction a nightmare. Added protection from the various governors and local politicians made it almost untouchable no matter what went on there.

"This place looks a little better." Jefferson got out of the Jeep and looked around. "But it still smells bad."

"I've been told that no amount of bleach can get rid of that smell," Sharyn replied. "I know the carpets inside are like walking on a cesspool."

"You could've taken me some place nice for lunch," he joked. "I've got plenty of places like this in my own jurisdiction."

"The food is bad." She knocked hard on the locked front entrance. "But the company is even worse."

She half expected to see Marti poke his head around the door to see what she wanted as he had the last time she was out here. Instead, Barker was there in jeans and a plaid flannel shirt. "Can I help you, Sheriff?"

This place, and the way Barker got it, left a bad taste in Sharyn's mouth. It was legal, but just barely so. If it would have been up to her, she would've burned the place to the ground. Probably half of the complaint calls in the county on a Friday night came from out here. "Barker," she acknowledged him. "I'd like to talk to Marti."

"He's not here. I caught him thieving the second week I had the place. He's been gone since then."

She nodded, glancing around. "Any idea where he went?"

"Nope. I don't want to know either. Little weasel."

Sharyn gave him her card. "Call me if you hear anything. I have a few questions for him."

"I'll do that, Sheriff." Barker looked at her card. "Would you two like something to drink since you came all the way out here?"

"No, thanks." She smiled. "But you've done a lot of work out here. The place almost looks decent."

"I know some bad blood went into getting back what rightfully belonged to my family," he defended. "But I want to make this place presentable. It doesn't have to be the kind of place it's always been."

"Good luck with that." She turned to walk back to the Jeep. "Something isn't right," she said to Jefferson in a low voice.

He agreed. "I think that little weasel might still be here."

"You drive." She handed him her keys. "Circle around and drop me off at the back of the building. Let's see if he runs."

"So I don't get lunch and you get all the fun?"

She laughed. "This *is* my county after all."

Jefferson drove the Jeep slowly around the building like they were checking out the place. Sharyn jumped out behind the storehouse that used to hold bootleg whiskey. Jefferson kept going toward the main road back to town as though they hadn't found anything wrong.

Sharyn crept up to the back of the nightclub, drawing her revolver when she heard loud voices coming from the building. Up close, she could see the work Barker had done was mostly a cover of cheap paint and replacing a few missing boards. It was whitewash, like telling her Marti was gone.

She hid behind an old barrel that caught rain from the roof and waited as the back door opened.

"I said you could stay here as long as you didn't get

in trouble." Barker tossed a dirty green duffle bag out the door with Marti right behind it.

"I ain't in no trouble with the sheriff," Marti yelled back. "I haven't been into town in a week. I don't know what she was doing out here, but it didn't have nothin' to do with me."

"Then why was she asking for you? You get your stuff and get out of here."

"You can't run this place without me." Marti shook his fist at Barker. "You don't know the people I know. You won't last a week out here without me."

Sharyn stood up and leveled her weapon at him. "And that's exactly what I want to talk to you about. Down on your knees. Hands behind your head."

"Aww, Sheriff," Marti protested as he complied with her command. "We're old friends, right? I've helped you out plenty of times. Why do you want to come up and cause me trouble?"

"You and I have a mutual friend, Marti," she explained as she put handcuffs on him. "Jill Madison-Farmer. Remember her?"

Sharyn glanced up and noticed that Barker wasn't in the doorway anymore. She knew he couldn't be stupid enough to try to help Marti. But a sense of presence behind her and a shadow on the side of the building told its own story.

As she turned from cuffing Marti, she kicked out and to the side where she caught the glimpse of shadow.

Someone grunted when her foot came in contact with soft belly tissue. Marti was still on his knees as she glanced behind her to see Barker drop a large piece of two-by-four. "That was stupid," she said. "I guess you've already been out here too long."

When Jefferson came around the corner with his gun drawn, he nodded toward the path that led between the storehouse and the nightclub. "I'll take care of this one, but I think the other one's getting away."

Sharyn looked back at where Marti had been. He was gone, but not far. He ran down the path, slipping and sliding in the mud left over from the snow. Before she even started after him, he'd fallen face down and was having a hard time getting up.

She picked him up by his jacket collar and pushed him to his feet in front of her. "That was even more stupid. I said I just wanted to talk."

"You didn't come out here to talk," Marti whined, covered in mud. "You already *know*."

"You're right. I do." She read him his rights. "You want to make this easier on yourself?"

"Yes, ma'am."

"Tell me where your friend Ronnie Shaefer is and I'll do what I can for you."

"I don't know anybody by that name."

She sighed. "That's too bad. I hear they're having trouble with the heat out at the county jail. I hope you have some warm clothes."

"Maybe I could ask around," Marti offered. "I don't know this Shaefer guy, but maybe one of my friends do. You let me go in town for a while and I'll see what I can find out."

"How about you take me to Shaefer and I won't kick your butt from here to that cornfield?"

Marti looked out at the frozen brown stalks left in the field from last year's crop. "Sheriff, it's not nice to rat out your friends."

"I thought you didn't know him." She flicked a piece of cornstalk from her arm. "You better get your story straight before I introduce you as a kidnapper, drug dealer, and whatever else I can think of to throw in for a judge."

"Kidnapper?" He stared at her with fear in his eyes for the first time. "What are you talking about?"

"I'm talking about what you and your friend Shaefer did to Jill Farmer. Kidnapping is a federal offense. Lucky for you, the FBI is in town. They can take you right to a federal prison and you can avoid county lockup."

Marti whined. "Please don't let them take me. This is my home. I'd rather be in county lockup, Sheriff. I know plenty of people down there. I'm a loser, but I'm not federal. Don't let them take me."

Sharyn glanced up and Jefferson smiled at her, holding his own prisoner. "Maybe we have something to talk about after all."

*   *   *

Marti told them exactly where to find Shaefer. Sharyn and Jefferson left their two prisoners in the short-term lockup located in the basement of the courthouse. They set out again with less consequences as they found Shaefer asleep in his motel room on the interstate. They brought him back and put him in the interrogation room as Ed and Ernie watched with unspoken questions.

Sharyn ignored them until she gave Jefferson the paperwork he needed for his prisoner exchange. "Thanks again for your help."

"I enjoyed it. Let me know when you need me again." He flashed a white smile at her and nodded to Ernie and Ed as he left the office.

Ernie put down his cup of coffee. "We caught that dog they were worried about."

"That's good. I hope no one was hurt," Sharyn said.

"No one was hurt. In fact, it was a pack of dogs. It took me and Ed, Sam, and Bruce to get them in the truck."

"I'm glad there wasn't a problem," she answered absently.

He nodded toward the interrogation room. "What is *he* doing here?"

"Jefferson and I arrested him and Marti Martin for kidnapping and drug dealing. They were listed in Michaelson's computer. Jack hired them to get Jill off his back."

"And you didn't wait for *us*?" Ed asked. "Trudy called us. You could've waited."

Sharyn looked up. "I would've waited if Jefferson

hadn't shown up. Since he did, I thought I might as well take care of it."

Ed shook his head, blond curls plastered to his forehead with sweat. "So you're not really after Shaefer and Martin. You want Jack out of this. Has it struck you yet that he might not like his fiancée throwing him in jail?"

Trudy made a rude noise that expressed her feelings on the subject. Ernie asked Sharyn to come outside with him. "I think there's something we need to discuss."

They walked up the basement stairs and stood in the weak sunshine, cold wind tugging at their hair and clothes.

"This is never gonna get Jack," he advised her.

"It's federal," she told him. "It's exactly what we need."

"Yeah, if the two of them agree to testify."

"We only need one of them," she reminded him.

"When he finds out you're after him, that you've been playing him for a fool, you better plan on going on vacation. You won't be safe here."

"I'm not scared of Jack. If we can get Marti or Shaefer to testify, I'll take this to Mr. Percy. We can finally bring the truth out about Jack and put him away."

Ernie's face was angry when he put a hand on both of her shoulders. "I don't want to lose you like I did your daddy. Put this laptop thing behind you. Let it go. Or give it to the feds. Let them take care of it."

"You know I'm not going to do that."

He swore. It was the first time Sharyn had ever heard him use that language. "You're stubborn and head-strong. This can't come to any good."

She smiled at him. "It'll be okay. You'll see. We don't have to tolerate the kind of bad Jack is. Not when we have him where we want him."

"This is a mess for sure. Mark my words—there will be more to it than getting Marti to testify."

Sharyn knew her words wouldn't reassure him. She also knew she was going through with her plan. She leaned forward and hugged him. "We can do this, Ernie. We can get the man who killed my father and so many others. Help me."

He played with his frozen mustache. "It doesn't seem like I have much choice, does it? Okay. Let's go inside before we freeze."

Ed was watching Shaefer through the small window in the door. "I wish Joe was here. He could sweat a man better than anyone I ever knew."

"We'll have to make do without him." Sharyn opened the door. "Wish me luck."

She and Ed both went in to have a talk with Shaefer. The little man in the ragged clothes defied them, telling them over and over that he had no idea what they were talking about. "I don't even know Senator Winter. Leave me alone. Arrest me if you want to. Then I can get some sleep."

"That's gonna be a lot of sleep," Ed told him. "I

don't think they let anyone sleep that much in a federal prison. I think they want you to fraternize with the other boys. I think you'll get along just fine there."

"You don't scare me." Shaefer twisted up his mouth. "If you really had something, you'd have me behind bars already. You want something. I know. I've seen that look before."

Sharyn leaned her hands on the table, her face very close to his. "I want you to understand something. I don't care what happens to *you*. I want the man who paid you to ruin Jill Madison-Farmer's life."

Shaefer's face went white, but he laughed. "You're not getting that from me. Put me in prison. I don't care."

"I have this theory," she said. "I think you and Marti have been Jack Winter's paid hands in this town for a long time. Probably since before he had you kill my father."

He came halfway up out of the chair. "Wait a minute. I was talking about that big-mouth lawyer. I didn't say anything about killing the sheriff. I didn't *kill* anybody. Killing the sheriff, that's a death sentence. I'm scared of needles."

Sharyn glanced at Ed. "I think we can find evidence that will prove you killed my father *and* kidnapped Jill Madison-Farmer. Maybe we can even find a few other things to throw in."

Shaefer tried to stand up, but Ed's hands pushed him back down. "You can't pin that on me. I'll testify to that. I didn't kill the sheriff. I don't know about Marti. He might be mixed up in that, but not me."

"He told us the same thing about you," Ed replied. "I don't know which one of you to believe. Maybe we'll just assume you acted together on orders from Jack Winter."

"He only told us to get that girl out of the way. He must've told someone else to kill Sheriff Howard. It wasn't me."

Sharyn stared at him, her face stony and unyielding. "Are you willing to testify to that?"

"I'll testify that I didn't have anything to do with the sheriff's death," Shaefer hedged. "That's all I'm saying."

"You just told us Jack hired you to get Jill Madison-Farmer out of the way," she reminded him. "You can't have it both ways."

"I'm not saying anything else." He wrapped his bony arms around his dirty frame.

"That's okay. That's all we needed to hear," Ed told him. "Now we can pretty you up and put you on the witness stand."

"He'll kill me," Shaefer blubbered. "And not in a good way."

"I hear sometimes they don't give you enough painkiller at the prison," Ed said to Sharyn. "And sometimes they have to give you those drugs that stop your heart two or three times before you're really dead. Have you ever heard that?"

"All right!" Shaefer screamed. "All right. I'll testify. But you better put me some place real safe or Jack will kill me before you ever get me to court."

Sharyn nodded, a strange feeling of contentment settling in her chest. "Don't worry. We'll take *real* good care of you."

Trudy typed up the account of how Jack hired Marti and Shaefer to kidnap, drug, and frame Jill Madison-Farmer. It was quiet in the office the entire time he was speaking. No phones rang and no one came into the basement. It was as though the world around them realized they were doing something momentous. Something that would change Diamond Springs and Montgomery County forever.

Sharyn made copies of what Trudy typed as Ernie put the taped version into their safe. The next step was evident. They would have to take this to Mr. Percy and have a judge issue an arrest warrant for Jack.

Ernie nodded at Sharyn. "Are you ready to do this?"

She took a deep breath. "I'm as ready as I'll ever be."

"What about me?" Shaefer demanded. "Don't you have to put me in protective custody or something before this hits the paper and everyone knows?"

"You'll be in protective custody," Ed told him. "The jail is as protective as you could want. Been in there myself. It's not a bad place and the food isn't half bad either."

"That won't stop Jack." Shaefer laughed. "He'll find somebody to kill me in there. Like he found me and Marti to do that other thing."

"The FBI will pick you up before we pick Jack up," Sharyn promised as she opened her cell phone to call Agent Brewster. "You'll be safe. All of this doesn't mean anything to us without you."

Ernie patted him on the back. "That's right, old son. We at least have to keep you alive until you testify."

Despite Shaefer's wailing, Ed led him to the lockup while Sharyn and Ernie walked upstairs to talk to Mr. Percy. Agent Brewster wasn't sure about moving on Jack so quickly despite the evidence they found in Michaelson's laptop.

Sharyn disagreed. "He already suspects something since he found out you're out there searching Michaelson's house."

Brewster swore. "How did he find out? I have three agents out here that I would trust with my life. There's no way they told him."

"Maybe it was whoever you report to. I assume you filed some kind of document allowing you to do this. Jack knows a lot of people. It probably wasn't hard to figure out."

"Then he must be getting nervous about the laptop," Brewster surmised. "Because we haven't been able to find anything to link him to Michaelson's death. We found a few interesting items you'll want to look at. But nothing to do with Jack."

Sharyn asked him to take Marti and Shaefer into protective custody, possibly getting them out of Diamond Springs. "I'm on my way to get an arrest warrant for Jack. Everything will blow up after that."

He agreed. "Let me know what I can do to help. We have to make this stick. We may never have this opportunity again."

Closing her cell phone outside of Mr. Percy's office door, Sharyn looked at Ernie. "This is it."

He squeezed her hand. "It is. I hate to think what all will crawl out of the woodwork after this, but here we go."

Sharyn knocked on the solid wooden door and Percy called for her to enter. She opened the door and saw Jack standing behind the DA. He smiled as she walked into the room.

Chapter Eleven

Sharyn hoped she didn't appear as trapped and frustrated as she felt. It was like the old days when Jack was DA and she had to come to him, knowing he was behind so much of what she was fighting against.

He stood there smugly smiling at her, pale blue eyes mocking her, as though he knew every move she was going to make before she made it. Justice had nothing to do with the rage she felt. Her hand that held the documents trembled to hold her grandfather's revolver instead. The irony wasn't lost on her.

She forced herself to relax and take a deep breath. She'd played this game with him for years, since she took her father's job the day after he was killed. She could play it a little longer.

But what about Percy? She had never seen or heard anything about him being involved with Jack. There was no record of it by Michaelson, but that only went back so far. On the other hand, here Jack sat with Percy like old friends, possibly discussing the fact that she was on her way upstairs to have him arrested.

She glanced at Ernie. His gaze was glued on her. She knew he understood what she was going through and what she was thinking. Now she had to decide if she could trust Mr. Percy or if she should take the evidence she had to the state attorney general. If she made the wrong move, her whole effort could be wasted.

"What can I do for you, Sheriff?" Mr. Percy sat back in his chair and made a pyramid out of his hands as he studied her.

Sharyn made her choice. If it was wrong, she would live to regret it. But as always, she let her instinct guide her. "I have official department business to discuss with you, sir."

Her words implied the other man would have to leave. Percy swiveled his head to glance up at his companion. "I think she's asking you nicely to leave, Jack. Did you two have a spat?"

Jack chuckled. "Sharyn and I understand each other, Eldeon. We don't have spats, do we?"

"If you wouldn't mind excusing us." She nodded. "This won't take long."

Percy's eyebrows rose. "Sounds like trouble to me. You'd better go, Jack. I'll call you later."

The senator leisurely moved away from the desk. He stopped long enough to give Sharyn a quick kiss on the cheek before he left the room. Percy buzzed for Toby to join them. "Good to see you, Deputy Watkins. What's the fuss, Sheriff?"

When the young ADA had joined them and the door was closed behind him, Ernie and Sharyn sat down in front of Percy's immaculate desk. Even though it was winter, the ceiling fan moved overhead and the DA wore his trademark white linen suit.

"It was a hard decision to bring this to you, sir," Sharyn confided in him. "I remember my father had nothing but good to say about you when he was alive. Ernie is the same way. I'm sure he'd lay down his life for you because of your work with the veterans in our community. I respected my father's judgments, even though some of them were wrong. I respect Ernie. That's why I decided to bring this to you instead of taking it to the attorney general."

Percy's gaze was diamond-hard. "I appreciate your sincerity, Sheriff. You have quite a way of giving a compliment with one hand while you stab me in the back with the other. However, I assume you have your reasons. Please enlighten me."

She put the paperwork in front of him without speaking. He put on his glasses and read through the information. The furrow between his brows deepened as he read.

Finally he looked up. "This is pretty strong stuff. I hope you know what you're doing."

"I hope so too." She explained about Michaelson's laptop that they found in his home. "It has enough evidence to hang Jack, including evidence linking him to my father's death."

"I'm not a defense attorney any longer, young woman, but if I were, I would question the validity of Mr. Michaelson's statements. How do we know he didn't have a vendetta against Jack? How do we know this whole suicide wasn't set up with the information to cause trouble? Maybe Mr. Michaelson had a falling out with Senator Winter. It wouldn't be the first time something of that nature occurred."

Sharyn put her second document in front of him. "I thought of that too, sir. I wouldn't bring you these charges, especially against Jack, if I didn't have corroboration."

He read through Shaefer's confession and shook his head. "You know I always wondered what happened to Ms. Madison-Farmer. She was a promising defense attorney. I approached her several times about working for my firm."

"She was helping me." Sharyn told him about the call from State Prison implicating Jack in her father's death.

"Jill came too close to something Jack didn't want her to find. He had Shaefer and Martin do his dirty work. The theme runs through Michaelson's information."

Percy sighed and removed his glasses, sitting back and closing his eyes as he pyramided his hands together. "I've been friends with Jack Winter for many years. I suspect you know that and that's why you suggested I might be corrupt in this matter. I've been worried for some time that he had crossed over the line." He opened his eyes, his gaze piercing into Sharyn's. "No one is above the law, Sheriff. Not you. Not me. Not Jack. I'll get you the necessary warrants you need for this. But I want a copy of Michaelson's hard drive on my desk this afternoon. This is going to be a royal stink."

"Reminiscent of Mr. Talbot." Ernie nodded. "What is it with the people we elect to represent us up there?"

"Sometimes," Mr. Percy ruminated, "a man forgets who he is and where he's from. On that day, anything is possible." He stood up and offered Sharyn his hand. "Thank you for coming to me with this, Sheriff."

"I appreciate your honesty, sir. I'll get you that information."

"She just doesn't know you the way I do," Ernie said to him. "I know you'll do what's right."

Toby nodded to them before they left the DA's office. Ernie's eyes narrowed on his eager, young face as he walked by him. When he and Sharyn were alone in the hall, he shook his head. "You know, I hate this business sometimes."

Sharyn glanced back at the door to the DA's office. "You think there's a problem after all?"

"I'm afraid I do." He took out his gun and double backed to the office they'd just left.

"*You* can't shoot him if I can't shoot him," Sharyn told him softly. "What are you doing?"

Ernie didn't reply. He slowly opened the door and crept into the small outer office. The inside door to Percy's office was closed. ADA Fisher was at his desk, the phone in his hand. He didn't move or look up until Ernie put the barrel of his gun against his neck. "Easy, son. Let's not do anything either of us will regret. Cari is gonna be mad enough at me without me shooting you."

Toby let the phone receiver drop out of his hand. He didn't move as Sharyn retrieved the phone from the carpeted floor. She put the phone to her ear in time to hear a voice say, "Senator Winter's office. How may I help you?"

She was about to put the phone down on the base when Percy stepped out of his office. "What *is* going on out here, Sheriff? Deputy, put that weapon away. What are you doing?"

Ernie took his handcuffs from his belt. "I believe I'm arresting your assistant, sir."

Sharyn handed the phone to Mr. Percy. "All these

years, I've known it was someone. I just didn't know who. First it was Michaelson working for Jack then I guess it was you, Toby."

"I want an attorney," Fisher said immediately. "I want one now."

Percy eyed his assistant with something like revulsion. "You'll get your lawyer, young man. Lucky for you the system doesn't allow for me to give you my shoe across your butt as well."

Fisher looked at him mutinously but never said a word. Sharyn couldn't believe it. She knew Cari wouldn't believe it. "You are going to be unpopular," she said to Ernie.

"With everyone but Terry." Ernie smiled his half smile. "Okay, on your feet," he said to Toby. "You have the right to remain silent, which I can see you understand."

While Ernie read him his rights, Sharyn turned to Percy. "I don't think he had a chance to say anything to Jack. Does this affect your decision?"

"In a way." Percy smoothed an imaginary wrinkle from his white suit coat. "I thought I was going home early today with the weather and all. Instead, I think I'll accompany you to serve your warrant on Jack. Bad news is best shared with friends."

Three hours later, Sharyn, Ernie, and Mr. Percy were riding in what had become a parade of vehicles approaching Jack's home on Diamond Lake. The media had somehow found out about the warrant for Jack's arrest and were waiting for them to leave the courthouse. They had nothing to say to the TV cameras or the shouted questions from Foster Odom, lead reporter for the *Diamond Springs Gazette.*

Because the FBI was involved in the case, Agent Brewster and another agent on his staff accompanied them in another car. The parade went down Main Street to First Avenue and turned left. People on the sidewalks watched as they went by.

It ended at Jack's front door. He was waiting for them, chatting with Jimmy Dalton, the owner and publisher of the *Gazette* and a pretty, blond reporter from News 14. He looked more like a man at a party than someone about to go to jail.

The crowd that had slowly built up around the senator's house turned to face the long line of cars that swung into his driveway. Reporters rushed forward when they saw Mr. Percy get out of the car. Sharyn and Ernie followed him, but the press was focused on the DA.

Percy stepped aside for Sharyn to serve Jack the arrest warrant. Another warrant allowed them to search his home and office. Sharyn gave him both documents. Ernie stepped behind him to take his arm. Anyone else would have left the scene in handcuffs, but a senator was different.

Jack shook his head at Sharyn, ignoring Ernie. "I can

see you've been busy. I should have insisted on you taking my ring so you wouldn't have so much time to get into trouble."

"You and I were never real enough to go that far," she told him, conscious of the TV cameras and reporters.

"Don't say that, sweetie. You and I were meant to be together. Let's talk about it over dinner tonight."

"I don't eat dinner in jail. Give me a call when you get out."

"Who said anything about jail?" He winked at her. "Pick you up around eight?"

"Let's go." Ernie urged him toward the car. He began telling the senator his rights as they walked.

"You don't have to bother with that, Deputy. I think I know my rights better than you do."

The crowd crushed in closer as they moved toward the car. Sharyn opened the back door and Ernie pushed Jack inside with a little more force than was necessary.

"I'll take him back and get him settled in," Ernie said to Sharyn. "You ride back with Mr. Percy."

Brewster and his agent stood to one side watching the crowd. He approached Sharyn before she reached the DA's car. "Looks like a good job. I hope we can make it stick."

"We will. You said you have something for me from Michaelson's house?" Before he could answer, her cell phone rang. She apologized for the interruption then answered it.

"I see you're busy," Nick said. "But I think I have something you might be interested in."

"Are you back at work?"

"Would I be calling you if I wasn't?"

Sharyn swallowed hard on that small bite. "What is it, Nick?"

"A hiker found, or re-found, Michelle Frey's body up on Palmer Mountain. They brought her in about an hour ago. She's pretty torn up, but some things are more difficult to get rid of. Ms. Frey was pregnant."

"I'll be over there as soon as I can." Sharyn closed her cell phone and faced Brewster. "They found my hit-and-run victim that was taken from the ME's lab. I have to go."

He nodded. "I'll leave that information at your office. Call me when you have a chance to look at it. Good luck, Sheriff."

The crowd began to break up once Jack was gone. The media moved to the courthouse to get as much information as they could. Sharyn got in the DA's big, white Cadillac and asked him to drop her off at the hospital.

Mr. Percy warned of political repercussions brought on by Jack's arrest. "Whether you like it or not, your name has been linked with his. You may pay a price for it when it's time for reelection."

She didn't argue with him on that point. "That may be. But it sure made me feel a lot better."

"I'm assuming your relationship with him these past

few months was simply a ruse. I hope it was worth the consequences."

Sharyn told him about Agent Brewster's plan. "It wasn't necessary anyway, but there was no way to know we would find Michaelson's evidence."

"A trifle misguided, but admirable." Percy stopped at the end of the hospital parking lot. "Good work, Sheriff. I hope this changes the dynamics of the town."

Sharyn said good-bye and went down the steps into the morgue. It was cooler in here with no sunlight to promise warmth. Megan flashed her a hateful look as she walked by. Keith said good morning and pointed her toward Nick.

"That was some interesting television." Nick looked up from the sink where he was washing his hands. "You got your man."

"I did." She wished she hadn't paid such a terrible price to do it. Spending the last few months with Jack had been hard. No amount of soap and water could wash away that feeling. She had let him near her, not just physically, but mentally, all the time knowing what he was. "You said Michelle was pregnant. Was the baby Michaelson's?"

"No. That's what I thought too. He got her pregnant, didn't want to face the consequences, yada yada yada. But Michaelson wasn't the baby's father."

"Who else?" She paced the tile floor restlessly. "I guess I'll have another talk with her ex-husband."

He nodded. "You'll have to get me permission for a blood test. That's the only way we'll know for sure."

"What about Michaelson?" She studied the bruises on Nick's face and watched him limp across the room to get a file. It hurt to see it. She hoped he wasn't back at work too soon.

"Like I told you, he died from carbon monoxide poisoning. Case closed. The only thing I found that might be considered strange is a bruise around his neck."

Sharyn considered his words. "What does that mean? What kind of bruise? Did someone incapacitate him before he died?"

"No. I think it was made by a chain I found on the seat beside him. It was like he pulled it too hard against his neck. He definitely wasn't killed with it."

"But it might have been used to hold him in place?"

"Possible. It was a nice chain, sturdy enough to do the job. Someone could have used it to keep him from trying to escape. Strangulation to the point of unconsciousness." He looked up from his notes. "But if you're looking for a little sign that pops out saying Jack killed me, I didn't find that. The kids haven't found anything else in the Hummer and Brewster told me he didn't find anything in his search of the house and garage."

"Maybe we'll find something as we search Jack's house and office. Anything else on the girl?"

"Nothing that stood out. Have you been through her house yet?"

"In a cursory way." Sharyn was ready to go. She was beginning to feel awkward talking to him when they seemed to have nothing to say. "We'll go back out there and I'll call you if we find anything."

"Great." He took off his glasses. "Sharyn, maybe we should . . ."

Her phone rang in time so she didn't have to deal with whatever he was going to say. It was Chief Tarnower. "Sheriff, Senator Winter got away from your man at the courthouse. They took your deputy to the hospital. I've got some men out looking for the senator, but no sign of him yet."

"What happened?"

"It appears the senator had someone waiting at the courthouse. Your deputy tried to walk him inside to the lockup. He was assaulted by Winter's accomplice and they both got away."

She couldn't believe it. She immediately thought of the man she felt sure assaulted Nick at the lab. "How bad was Ernie hurt?"

"Didn't look too bad to me. Watkins has a hard head anyway. I'm sure he'll be okay." The chief cleared his throat and broached another topic. "By the by, Sheriff, I don't appreciate being left out of that high-profile arrest that happened in my jurisdiction. I realize you did the legwork on it with your FBI friends, but I would have appreciated at least a heads up on the matter."

Almost too busy thinking about Ernie and where

Jack could be, she promised to include him next time. It hadn't been that long since she was sheriff of both Diamond Springs and Montgomery County. Old habits died hard.

"What happened now?" Nick asked as she closed her cell phone.

She explained about Jack and Ernie. "I have to go. If Jack gets out of the county, we might never find him again."

Nick grabbed her arm as she turned to leave. "Be careful, Sharyn. He could come after you. Nobody likes to look like a fool."

"I will. I'll call if I hear anything."

Within twenty minutes of his escape, there was an APB out on Jack along with dogs and helicopters searching for him in the area. The airports, bus, and train stations were alerted. He was a public figure with a recognizable face. Sharyn felt sure it wouldn't take long to get a lead on him.

In the meantime, Brewster and his agents were searching Jack's house and office. Another team was searching his senate office. Sharyn was eager to find out who Jack's accomplice was. He was the senator's strong right arm. Could he have been involved in Michaelson's death?

Sharyn had Trudy call in volunteer deputies to help with the search. Marvella and JP, Cari and Terry, were all called in early to help run the operation. Cari couldn't believe it when she heard Toby was in jail for being Jack's informer. Terry actually thanked Sharyn for putting the ADA there to further his cause with Cari. In a moment between phone calls, Sharyn considered it was definitely best to separate the two deputies. There was bound to be trouble there.

She was surprised to look up and see Joe coming down the ramp in his wheelchair. His black gloves and signature dark glasses were in place, along with his uniform. "I thought you could use an extra hand," he said. "I know I can't chase anyone down yet, but I can answer the phone and take care of other problems. You need me here, Sheriff."

Sharyn smiled. "You're right. Grab a phone and get started. We're trying to find out which way Jack left the courthouse."

While they were waiting to hear updates on Jack, Sharyn sent Marvella and JP to Michelle's house. "I want you to look at everything. There may be something important that we're missing." She explained about the young woman being pregnant.

Marvella frowned. "What exactly are we looking for? I thought she died in the street?"

"We missed something since we didn't know she was pregnant. Look for anything that can give us details about her life. This isn't as simple as it sounded to begin with. I need to know who that baby's father is."

"We could check clinics too," JP said. "Maybe she knew she was pregnant and went to the doctor."

"Sounds good." Sharyn nodded. "Keep your radios on. We might need you if we find Jack."

"What have you heard about Ernie?" Marvella asked. "I can't believe he let someone sneak up on him like that."

"Me either," Sharyn agreed. "The doctor says he'll be fine. We'll have to get along without him for at least today. In the meantime, you two find me something important at Michelle's house. I want to tie this thing up."

"You got it, Sheriff." Marvella grabbed her coat. "Come on, JP. Let's go find us something important."

Sharyn watched them go then sat down at her desk. The FBI evidence bag with Michaelson's name on it was waiting for her. She ignored the phones and the buzz of voices in the room and opened it. She wasn't expecting to find anything important in it.

Michaelson's watch was in the bag. There was a phone message on his answering machine, according to Brewster. They checked it out and found that the call came from State Prison in Raleigh. Brewster suggested in a note that it could be from a client he was representing.

There were a few pictures in the folder. One of them was marked as Michaelson and his sister. Sharyn looked up her name and address. She didn't realize Michaelson had any next of kin. She hoped his sister didn't have to hear about his death on the news. Since she was living in Oakland, California, she doubted it. Finding out about his sister amazed Sharyn since there was no other reference to her.

Another photo made Sharyn sit up, her mind calculating the possibilities. It was a photo of Michaelson and Julia Richmond, an ex-county commissioner she'd arrested for murder. It was recent. Julia was wearing a prison uniform. Was Michaelson representing her? Was that where the prison call came from?

The next picture was of the two of them kissing. Obviously not just a business relationship. So, Michaelson was having conjugal prison visits with Julia and spending time with Michelle. He was a busy man.

Sharyn didn't waste any time. She called the sheriff's office in Oakland and apprised him of the situation. He told her he would send someone out to talk to Michaelson's sister. Sharyn thanked him then got on the phone with the warden in Raleigh and set up a phone interview with Julia.

Julia was tearful and upset when she talked to her. She'd heard about Michaelson's death and freely conversed with Sharyn about their relationship. "We were seeing each other before you put me in here, Sheriff. I let my father talk me out of Alan representing me at the trial. That was a big mistake. Alan was preparing my appeal. He was everything to me."

Sharyn waited while Julia stopped sobbing. "You saw him on a regular basis at the prison?"

"Yes. He was up here last week. He told me he had some information he was going to trade for my freedom. He didn't tell me what it was. I don't know if it involved my case or not. He's gone now so I guess it doesn't matter."

That's why he was storing up information on the good-old-boy network. Sharyn made note of it, but didn't mention it to Julia. Michaelson was going to use his contacts with Jack and the others to trade for his lover. "When was the last time you talked to him?"

"From what I read in the paper, a few hours before he died. He called me and we talked for a while."

"Did he mention a woman named Michelle Frey?"

"No. Who is she?"

"We think Michaelson killed her. She was pregnant and had a young son as well. We thought the baby might be his, but we know now that it wasn't."

"There's no way. Alan wouldn't do anything like that. He didn't kill that girl. And he couldn't get her pregnant even if he wanted to."

"Why is that?" Sharyn doodled on a piece of paper, thinking that women were always too gullible where men were concerned.

"Because he had a vasectomy years ago. He might have been seeing someone else, though I don't believe that. Alan loved me. But no matter what, he didn't get her pregnant."

Sharyn thanked her for her time and promised to let her know if there was any update in the case. She understood now why Michaelson created the computer log of illegal activity, particularly around Jack. He was going to give them a dirty senator in exchange for his girlfriend's freedom. Who knows? The state might even have taken it.

But if Michaelson wasn't dating Michelle, why was he spending so much time with her? There was no doubt in Nick's mind that Michaelson's Hummer killed Michelle. But what if *he* wasn't driving it? And what if someone else was also dating the woman?

It was a lot of questions with no answers. Her phone rang. It was Marvella. "I don't know for sure if this is anything, Sheriff, but we found a bunch of receipts for the Super Eight Motel up on the interstate. There's a bunch of money here too. If she was meeting someone there, he was paying her and she paid the motel bills. Maybe her lover was trying to stay anonymous."

"Meet me there." Sharyn picked up her hat. "Bring the receipts."

The motel was quiet when Sharyn got there. Most of the guests were gone. A few housekeepers in blue uniforms were going from room to room trying to get the place cleaned up for the coming night.

Marvella and JP pulled in after her and got quickly

out of their vehicle. "We found some receipts for that restaurant too." JP nodded toward the small café beside the motel.

"Mostly breakfast and supper, if you know what I mean." Marvella rolled her eyes and moved her head from side to side to make her point.

"Let's go have a talk with Mr. Caywel," Sharyn suggested. "Maybe he noticed something unusual going on out here."

Chapter Twelve

"**I** don't know her," Caywel said when Sharyn showed him Michelle's photo. "I never saw her here."

Marvella narrowed her eyes. "Funny that we have so many receipts from her being here, isn't it?"

"I'm not here every minute of every day," Caywel said. "I have a night clerk."

"You'd better bring him in then," JP told him. "How about a black Hummer? Have you ever seen one of those here?"

"No. We don't get any of those here. People with money tend to stay in town."

"Better call that night clerk." Marvella walked toward the check-in desk. "Oooh! Look! They have HBO. I wish I'd known that last month when my sister was visiting.

She could've stayed out here. All she cared about was watching the TV anyway."

Caywel looked uncomfortable. "Sheriff, I can't just bring in my night clerk. The boy has to get some sleep. I'll tell him he needs to come see you when he gets off shift tomorrow."

"I'm afraid that's not good enough, sir," Sharyn said. "There are two people who are dead and we have to find out what happened to them. If you could call in your night clerk, I'd appreciate it."

"Your daddy would never do me this way," the motel owner accused. "He knew I was a man of my word."

"I'm sorry, Mr. Caywel, but that isn't going to help. If you can't call in someone else who might recognize these receipts, you'll have to come back to Diamond Springs with us."

The man stared at her for an instant then took off in a sprint down a hill behind the motel that led to a strip of jack pines and gnarly old oak trees.

"Well I never!" Marvella put her hands on her hips. "Shoot him, JP. He's obviously guilty of something."

JP looked at Sharyn. "Sheriff?"

Sharyn took a deep breath. "Don't be crazy, JP. I know you know better. It's not like we think Caywel killed Michaelson or Frey. But he must have something he doesn't want to tell us."

JP smiled. "Shoot him in the leg so he can't run anymore?"

Marvella sighed. "No. She's telling us we have to run out after him. And me in my new shoes. I'll need a pedicure after this."

When both of her deputies were in hot pursuit, Sharyn got in her Jeep and drove up the barely discernable logging road that ran perpendicular to the line of trees. Loggers had been working the area for some time after it was announced that another strip mall would go up by the motel.

She waited, wondering what Caywel could possibly know that would be worth going to jail for. She watched him stick his head out of the trees, glancing back as he heard Marvella and JP coming after him. He didn't look Sharyn's way until she was on him.

Trusting that his luck was still with him, he turned to head back into the brush. Sharyn grabbed a broken tree limb and jammed it in front of his headlong flight. Caywel ran through it and fell face first into the red mud.

"Sheriff, I'm not saying anything. I don't care what you do to me. It can't be worse than what *he'll* do."

She pushed him down with her knee in his back and put handcuffs on him. "I don't know about that. Marvella has new shoes and she says she'll need some work done on her feet after chasing you. I've seen her shoot a man for less."

Caywel started crying and rubbed his hands on his dripping nose. Marvella and JP caught up with them.

Marvella was frowning and shaking her head while JP had his gun drawn.

"Sheriff," Caywel cried. "Don't let her hurt me."

Marvella pushed back her sassy new haircut and stared at the man. "Oh, I'm gonna hurt you, little man. You made me ruin my new shoes and I think I broke a nail back on one of those trees. And that's not going into detail on the bruise I feel forming on my hip."

Caywel blubbered a little louder. "It isn't my fault. I didn't want them at my motel. He insisted. He paid good, but not that good. Mostly, everyone knows Jack will kill you dead if you cross him."

Sharyn paused. "Are you saying Jack Winter was seeing Michelle Frey at the Super Eight?"

Marvella put her hand on Sharyn's shoulder. "Now don't get too worked up, Sheriff. I know he was dating you and spending time with her too, but he's well out of your life. I know a few men who would love to date you. You forget about that old barnacle. We'll find you someone better."

Sharyn ignored her and repeated the question. Caywel nodded. "He had Alan Michaelson drive them here so if anyone noticed it would look like he was with that girl instead of the senator. I'm sorry, Sheriff. If I would've known he was your boyfriend, I would've called you."

Maybe that made some sense. If Jack was hiding his affair with Michelle by using Michaelson to pick her up and bring her to the motel, he might be the father of her unborn baby. Did Michelle try to use that information to get attention or something more from her lover? Did Jack send Michaelson to kill her or did he go himself?

Her phone rang. It was Ed. "I think I got us a name and address on Jack's buddy that you were talking about." He gave her the address. "Where are you anyway?"

"Picking up an expert witness. I'll meet you there in ten minutes."

"What about me?" Caywel looked nervously between Sharyn and Marvella. "You can't tell Jack what I told you. I heard you never got him to jail. You'll never find him but he'll find me. You gotta get me out of the country. That's the only way I'll be safe. That man knows everyone."

"Take him back to the office for protective custody," Sharyn told Marvella and JP.

Marvella rolled her expressive dark eyes. "The jail is gonna get pretty full, Sheriff. Do you know what you're doing here or what?"

Sharyn laughed as she climbed back into her Jeep. "I hope so. Come on and get in. I'll take you back to the motel."

JP offered to go with her to meet Ed once they had dropped Caywel off at the courthouse. "You should not be alone, I think. The senator might be looking for you."

"I'll be fine. But thanks for volunteering. I have a

feeling Jack isn't hanging around to see what's going to happen next. Caywel is right. Jack has lots of powerful friends who owe him favors. We're doing the ground work, but it will surprise me if we ever get him in jail."

Sharyn left her deputies with Caywel at the motel and drove back to Diamond Springs to meet Ed. She called the hospital and was assured by a doctor that Ernie was going to be fine. He had a bump on the head, but was already angry that they bothered bringing him in. She thanked him for the information and turned down Main Street to get to the Regency Hotel.

At one time, this area of Diamond Springs was filled with wealthy tourists who came to drink the water that washed down from the mountains. They believed it would heal what was wrong with them. They built the old luxury hotel and the theater across the street. Many of their houses still overlooked Diamond Lake. The money and the parties were gone with the flappers and the gangsters, but the town continued to grow around what they had created.

Sharyn called ahead to let Terry's father, who managed the Regency Hotel, know they were coming. She knew he wasn't happy about his son joining the sheriff's department, but he was surprisingly pleasant and agreeable when she told him she needed to search one of the rooms. He even waived having a search warrant by giving her permission to search.

When she got there, she realized why. Terry was there with Ed. His father was all smiles, his hand on his son's shoulder.

"His name is Evan Harewood," Ed told her. "They call him Ace. He was released from State Prison about a month ago. We were lucky and caught him on surveillance tapes as he accompanied the senator around town. I've got Nick's kids checking anything at the lab for his fingerprints."

"He's in room four-seventy." Mr. Bartlett handed Terry the master key. "Please let me know if you need anything else from me."

"Thanks, Dad." Terry hugged his father briefly. "You better hang out in your office while we handle this. We don't want anyone getting hurt."

Bartlett was more worried about losing his only son. "Shouldn't you have shields or something like they have in New York?"

"We'll be fine," Terry assured him. "We have to go to work now."

When the hotel manager had scuttled back into his office, Terry pounded one black gloved fist into another. "Let's get him."

"Let's think about this." Sharyn stopped him. "There are two elevators and one set of stairs. I'll take the stairs. Each of you take an elevator. If Ace is here, I don't want him to leave without saying good-bye. I'm pretty sure he was the one who roughed up Nick and he could be Michelle and Michaelson's killer."

Ed nodded. "Take it easy, Terry. This guy is probably armed. He won't care if you're the law or not. He'll shoot first and worry about it later."

Terry smiled. "Okay. I'm ready. Let's go."

Sharyn shook her head and took out her revolver. "Keep in touch. If you see or hear anything strange, let us know."

Terry stepped into one elevator and Ed took the other. He waited until Terry was closed behind the metal door. "Maybe I spoke too quickly. Maybe I don't want him for a partner. I don't want anyone for a partner who's going to get me killed."

"He reminds me a lot of Joe. I'm sure he'll be fine."

The elevator door closed between her and Ed, but not before she heard him say, "Yeah, right."

She started slowly up the stairwell. The sunlight illuminated all of the corners, not allowing any shadows in the chilly space. She made her way to the first floor and paused. When she was sure it was clear, she went quietly up to the second floor.

She could only hope she wouldn't encounter any hotel guests who could be injured. Situations like this were too dangerous. She wouldn't be here if she thought there was another way.

The second and third floors were clear. There was no

word from Ed or Terry. She went cautiously up to the fourth floor. She reached for the door that opened into the hallway when Ed's voice came breathlessly over the radio. "He's here. I've got him pinned down in his room. I need you two up here. Where's Terry?"

Sharyn didn't answer. She ran down the long carpeted hallway where the 1920s crystal chandeliers showered prismatic colors as the sun hit them. There was no sign of Terry, but Ed kicked in the door to room four-seventy as she turned the corner.

A gunshot echoed from the room. It crossed the hall, striking the elevator door and bouncing off to shatter one of the crystals in the closest chandelier. Sharyn hugged the wall, but kept advancing toward the open door. She hoped Ed was all right. She didn't dare try to raise Terry on the radio until she knew the situation in the hotel room.

"Just missed him." Ed came back to the doorway. "He jumped out the window after he shot at me."

"Let's call for backup. I don't want to lose him now."

"Not a problem." The laugh lines fanned out from his deep blue eyes. "He dropped like a stone through one of those old fire escapes. I guess he thought he was in a movie or something. Nobody has used one of those for fifty years."

"You aren't hit or anything, are you?" Sharyn wondered at his placid demeanor. "We better get down there in case he's not hurt as bad as you think."

"My partner has him," Ed told her. "He's got a lousy sense of direction, but he ended up in the right place at the right time."

"You mean Terry went down to the basement instead of up here?"

"That's it. I'll make sure I do all the driving, but we'll be fine."

They put away their guns and glanced out the window that overlooked the alley behind the hotel. Terry had handcuffed the barely conscious man. He waved to them and Sharyn told him to call an ambulance. "I already took care of that, Sheriff," he responded. "Lucky for this boy that he fell on this old mattress out here. But I'm going to have to fine my dad for not disposing properly of trash."

Sharyn laughed. "I think you could give him a warning this time. Can you handle the situation down there?"

"I'm fine," he assured her. "You two take a look around up there and see what you can find."

She could tell he was as proud of himself as she was of him. Ed was already putting on latex gloves and looking through drawers in the old wardrobe, searching for whatever he could find that looked like it could help them.

The room was a mess of fast food wrappers and beer cans. Dirty clothes were everywhere. A half-eaten hamburger testified to how quickly Ace left the room when he realized they had found him.

"If this boy has been working for Jack, he's probably the one who helped him get away from Ernie," Ed said. "Why is he still here if Jack is gone?"

The question made Sharyn shiver, but she answered lightly, "Maybe Jack didn't need him anymore."

Ed lifted one blond brow. "And he left him *alive*? I don't think so."

Sharyn walked into the bathroom. There was no sign that Ace was planning on going anywhere. His razor and toiletries were still on the sink. There was a small pile of dirty clothes on the green tile floor. Some of them had large blood stains dried on the material. "I'm going to call Nick to come over and bag this stuff. This could be Nick's blood, for all we know."

"It sure isn't Ace's. That little girl out in Frog Meadow was an easy kill." Ed sniffed a partial cigar he found in an ashtray. "I doubt if Michaelson put up much of a fight either."

"But why kill Michaelson? Jack didn't know about the information on the computer or he would've taken it with him. If all he did was borrow Michaelson's Hummer, why kill him? Michaelson was too smart to give himself away over one person's death when he was so close to taking Jack down. It doesn't make sense."

She called the ME's office and talked to Keith, telling him they needed them at the hotel. The sound of sirens coming closer filled the room as she looked out the hotel window. Terry was holding a gun in his hand. He waved it at her with a big, dumb grin on his face.

"What's the correct procedure for handling evidence, Deputy?" she yelled out the window at him.

"Oh. Yeah." He hastily put on the gloves he had in his pocket. "Is that better?"

Sharyn didn't answer. Ed shook his head. "He's got some learning to do. No one's perfect, right?"

Terry went with the paramedics who took Ace to the hospital. Sharyn and Ed waited for Nick to get there. Once he was there, they could seal up the room until they had a chance to comb through everything.

Nick and Megan showed up a few minutes later. "Keith stayed behind so someone could hit *him* over the head if they want to break into the lab again," Nick explained when he saw Sharyn. "What happened here?"

"Not much." She explained about Ace as she handed him the blood-stained clothes she'd already bagged. "We were lucky. He must not have had time to get rid of these."

Nick's dark eyes were appreciative. "And I didn't get you anything."

"The blood on the clothes might be yours from the attack."

"A gruesome thought. Thanks."

"Where do you want me to start, Nick?" Megan leaned in close to him.

"Take the gun from the alley back to the lab and process it. I want to know where it came from and who shot it last."

Megan made a face at him. "We can do that when we get back. You need me here."

He looked up at her from contemplating the bloody clothes. "Did I give you some strange idea that this was a request? You work for me. Take the gun back to the lab. I'll call you when I'm done here."

Ed raised his eyebrows at Nick's curt tone with the girl. "I think I should head back to the office. You need a lift, Sheriff?"

"No. My Jeep is outside. If nothing urgent is happening, check in on Ernie, huh?"

"Sure thing." Ed glanced between her and Nick as Megan gathered her kit and left the room. "I'll just be going then."

There was silence between Sharyn and Nick as they were left alone in the room with the door closed. She watched him set up to collect evidence. She'd watched him repeat the steps many times. He was careful and deliberate. She thought it might have been that intense way he had of looking at things that attracted her to him in the first place.

"Can I help you do anything?" She knew the answer before she asked.

"No. That's okay. Thanks anyway."

"I guess I'll go then. It's been really busy the last few

days." She watched him limp across the room. "I hope you didn't come back too soon."

"This from a woman who had a house fall on her and wanted to go back to work the next day."

She couldn't argue with that. "I guess that's dedication."

"Or insanity."

"You know, you were right about me using my job to fall back on when I'm not sure what else to do about other parts of my life." She glanced up at him. He wasn't looking at her. Was he listening? "I was thinking about you the other night and I wasn't sure how to handle what's happened between us. So I got dressed and went to the office."

There was still no response. Sharyn waited another moment then turned to leave the room.

"It's easy to get lost in your work," he said finally. "I didn't know if it was day or night for ten years before I moved here."

"Nick, I'm sorry I hurt you. Maybe it was a stupid decision."

"*Maybe*?"

"Okay. It *was* a stupid decision. I didn't know Michaelson was setting Jack up to trade for Julia Richmond's release. I did what I thought I had to do."

He looked up at her. "I know. You're a good sheriff and a good person. Maybe too good. I wish I could pretend I'm not miserable without you because you scare me. There's no other way to say it. I think it might be the age difference. When you get older, you look at life differently."

"You aren't *that* old."

"I've aged a lot since I met you. I wish I could ask you to give up being sheriff and do what you planned to do before T. Raymond died. You would've been a good lawyer too."

"Thanks." *Is he going to ask me to give up my badge as part of an agreement for us to get back together?*

"But I can't." He smiled. "Would you? If the only way we could be happy together meant you couldn't be sheriff? Would you give up your badge?"

Sharyn stared straight into his eyes. "You wouldn't love me if I answered yes to that."

He shrugged. "You can't blame me for trying."

She didn't know if that meant they could be together or not. She couldn't ask. She wanted to be honest with him. She loved him, but she was who she was. She would have been different if she'd never seen her father lying dead on the floor of that convenience store where she bought popsicles as a kid. But she couldn't take that back.

Nick took off his gloves. "Could you step into the hall for a minute?"

She couldn't believe he would suddenly want to see where the bullet from Ace's gun went in the middle of this personal conversation, but she couldn't imagine any other reason for his request. It had to mean they were truly separated. He was reverting back to their professional relationship being all they had together.

Hurt and angry, she snatched open the hotel room door and let it slap against the wall. She took off her gloves and dropped them into a trash can. "I think the bullet ricocheted off the elevator door and hit that chandelier up there."

"I don't care."

She stopped pointing at the ceiling. "What do you mean?"

He put his arms around her. "I love you, Sharyn. Don't ever hurt me again like that. Okay?"

She blinked. "Okay."

They kissed, ignoring the ping of the opening elevator doors and the smiles on the faces of the hotel guests who passed them. Neither one noticed Mr. Bartlett until he had cleared his throat three times.

Sharyn opened her eyes and looked at the hotel manager across the top of Nick's shoulder. "Is there a problem, sir?"

"Excuse me, Sheriff. I don't mean to interrupt. How long will this room be out of commission? I'm only asking so I can tell housekeeping when to come back."

"Tell him I'll let him know," Nick whispered in her ear.

"The Medical Examiner's office will call you, sir."

"Thank you," Mr. Bartlett said. "I, uh, won't bother you again. Please carry on."

When he was gone, Sharyn and Nick both laughed.

"Do you think he really meant that about carrying on?" Nick asked.

"I hope so." She pressed her forehead to his. "Are we good now? Or do I have to do something else to make amends?"

"We're good." He kissed her again. "I can be done here in a couple of hours. How about you?"

"There's a fugitive on the loose and I can't quite pin down exactly why two people were murdered. What did you have in mind?"

"I was thinking about driving up into the mountains and watching the sunset. Then we could go back to my place and I'll cook something."

"Sounds good. I'll meet you at the courthouse. Call me when you're done here."

Sharyn left in a better frame of mind than she had been in for months. She and Nick were back together. Jack had finally been exposed as the demon he truly was. It was only a matter of time before someone turned him in or he was found. It probably wouldn't be in Diamond Springs, but the FBI would have him.

The office was in chaos when she got back. A hundred different calls from as many different sources had Jack spotted at everywhere from the airport in Charlotte to the bus station in Raleigh.

"Anything out of Ace at the hospital?" she asked Terry who was filling out reports.

"Nope. Jack has him well trained. He probably won't talk."

"I'll talk to Mr. Percy and see if we can cut Ace a deal. He could help us find Jack." Sharyn sat down and looked at her messages. There was nothing out of the ordinary. She tried to return a call from her Aunt Selma, but there was no answer.

She focused her attention on what evidence they had on the Michaelson/Frey murders. There hadn't been enough time to have any major forensic discovery back from Raleigh. The information she got from Julia might be valuable. Mr. Caywel said Jack was meeting Michelle at the motel. She had to conjecture that Jack was sleeping with the woman. If so, was it possible the child she carried was his?

They needed proof. She got on the computer and looked up Jack's history. He served in the military which could be a lead to his blood type and fingerprints. Even more interesting, when she contacted the military records database, she learned that Jack was also briefly in the CIA.

She called Brewster to update him on finding Ace and learning about Jack's intelligence background. The FBI agent was not surprised. "He was mustered out pretty quickly when he had a hard time passing the psyche tests. I didn't think it really pertained to the case or I would've told you."

"Does he still have contacts there?"

"Not that I know of. I think we should focus on this Ace character. If he killed for Jack, the chances are he has a pretty good idea where he is. They may even have set up a place to meet. Let's not miss this opportunity. I'll be there to help you question him in about an hour."

"All right. I'll see you then." Sharyn hung up the phone then changed her mind and tried her aunt's number again. There was still no response. It was odd because Selma had an answering machine. Maybe the power was out.

She called her mother who told her she hadn't heard from Selma all day. "I've heard some pretty disturbing things about Jack on television. Is it true he's going to prison?"

Sharyn could hear Caison's booming voice in the background saying that Jack would never go to prison. "He's too well connected. He'll slip through some small crack that no one is watching. Believe me; you'll never get that man behind bars."

Sharyn waited until he'd finished his tirade and asked her mother to put him on the phone. Faye offered to repeat a message to him but Sharyn insisted on talking to her future stepfather.

When she got him on the phone, she told him about the evidence against him on Michaelson's computer. "My advice to you would be to make a deal with the DA. Everyone wants Jack. You're in a position to help us.

This is going to blow Montgomery County wide open. I'm only giving you this heads up for my mother's sake."

There was silence for a long moment. Sharyn was afraid he might have had another heart attack. Then he finally said, "Thank you. I'll check into it."

With her mother standing there, he could hardly say more. Sharyn said good-bye and hung up. Caison could be the nail in Jack's coffin. He knew things that went on in the county before she was born. They had the information on the computer, but with Caison's corroboration it would seal the case.

There were a few others on the computer who might have been able to do the same thing. She admitted she was slightly prejudiced. She would never be happy with Caison taking her father's place, but she didn't have to be. Her mother was happy with him. That was all that mattered. She didn't know if he could get out of spending at least a little time in prison, but it was better than the rest of his life.

Her cell phone was beeping when she got off the phone with Caison. It was another call from Aunt Selma. She tried calling her aunt's cell phone number, but it went right to voice mail.

Sharyn tried calling Sam's cell phone, but there was no response there either. She called his partner in the wildlife service, Bruce Bellows, but Bruce was waiting for Sam on Diamond Mountain and hadn't heard from him all day.

A cold knot was beginning to form in Sharyn's stomach. She knew how angry Jack was that Aunt Selma was running for his Senate seat. Selma was so sure Jack couldn't hurt her. But that was only in the political arena. What if Jack wanted to have a last bit of revenge before he got out of town? He'd killed for less.

Ed and Terry had gone out on one last call before ending a twelve-hour shift and going home. Marvella and JP were out handling a domestic dispute. Joe started answering phones after Trudy went home. That only left Cari able to take any calls that came up. She couldn't take her.

Sharyn put on her hat and jacket, checked her revolver before she slipped it into her holster. She unlocked the gun storage and took a shotgun out, adding extra shells to her pocket.

"Are you planning on bringing Jack in by yourself?" Joe asked as he watched her.

"I'm going out to Selma's place," she answered, not denying his claim. "I think something might be wrong out there."

"Like what?"

"I don't know yet. I'll stay in touch."

"No, Sharyn. Take Cari with you." Joe's argument was undermined when a call came in for assistance from the highway patrol. Sharyn was walking out the door when he looked up again. He yelled her name, but the door closed behind her.

Chapter Thirteen

Sharyn parked her Jeep at the end of the driveway, blocking any exit. The day had been mostly overcast with deep clouds coming down from the mountains. The weather service was calling for more snow, but when she got out of her vehicle, there was no precipitation, just an ominous early darkness.

There were no lights on in the house or the barn where Selma and Sam did a lot of their work. Selma's car was missing from the drive along with Sam's truck.

Sharyn took a deep breath, relieved to see no one was there. It wasn't all that unusual for Sam and Selma to get wrapped up in their work and forget everything else. Sam was probably on his way up the mountain to meet Bruce. There was no telling where Selma was off to.

She started to get back in her Jeep when she noticed something out of place. The door to the barn was open. She knew there were expensive projects, both animal and plant, going on in the restored shelter. The colder weather could affect either of them.

It wasn't the life-threatening issue she was afraid she would find out there, but she couldn't leave until she took care of the problem. She knew her aunt would be devastated if she lost any of her plants.

Sharyn walked up to the top of the hill to close the barn door. The overhead light had come on in the strange twilight. She looked back at the house, but everything else seemed normal.

She secured the door after looking inside to make sure everything was okay. Her cell phone rang, startling her in the quiet. She glanced down to ID the caller and a sharp blow to the back of her head dropped her to her knees before she lost consciousness.

Her face was damp when she came to. Aunt Selma was wiping a wet rag across her forehead. "Sharyn? Can you hear me?"

"Yes." Her brain felt disconnected from her body, but she forced herself to focus. "What happened?"

Selma told her about Jack coming out to the house earlier in the day. He'd locked her in the basement. She didn't know where Sam was or if he was all right.

"Where is Jack now?" Sharyn sat up, her head throbbing, stomach threatening to heave.

"Always here for you, darling." The harsh overhead light came on and showed them his face. His clothes were dirty and disheveled. "I'm sorry you didn't come sooner. I tried all day to get you to come out here. Now it looks like we might have some snow. I hope there are enough supplies for us."

She didn't mention that Joe knew where she was going. When she didn't call in, he would send someone out after her. "I thought you'd be long gone by now. I can't believe you're stupid enough to still be in the county."

"That's exactly why I'm still here. No one thought to look for me here. But don't worry. We're not staying. I'm expecting a friend to fly in tonight and take me out of the country. Selma's road through the property should make a good landing strip. Then you and I are off for Argentina. I have a few friends down there in high places."

"I'm not going anywhere with you." She searched her pockets as she spoke. Her grandfather's revolver was gone, of course. The shotgun was in the Jeep. The shells were still in her pocket. She couldn't think what good that would do her.

"Get out of here and leave her alone," Selma snarled. "Haven't you ruined enough people's lives already?"

He laughed. "I didn't ruin anything. People do these things to themselves."

"What about Ace killing Michaelson for you after you had Michaelson kill Michelle Frey?" Sharyn asked. "How do you think they did that to themselves?"

"First of all, you have it wrong, Sheriff. In this case, your deductions are incorrect. I killed Michaelson myself. The man was taking advantage of a situation. As far as Michelle was concerned, I was hands on with that too. Matters of the heart require a personal touch, don't you think?"

"It's hard for me to believe even you are capable of killing your own child," Sharyn said. "Or didn't you know she was carrying your baby?"

He looked surprised. "I'm afraid you're mistaken there too, my dear. I guess I underestimated my effect on you. Michelle was carrying Michaelson's child. They fooled around a little on the side as he brought her to me. It's so hard to get decent help these days."

"You're mistaken, Senator." Sharyn shook her head. "Michaelson couldn't produce children. The child Michelle carried was *yours* before you killed it. Was that your first offspring? Somehow that seems appropriate to me. The world doesn't need to continue your seed."

"You don't know what you're talking about."

"You must've had some inkling, Jack," she scoffed. "You had her body stolen from the morgue. You weren't sure if it was yours or Michaelson's baby she carried, were you?"

He stepped forward abruptly and slapped her hard in

the face. The blow pushed her back against the wall. As he moved away from her, Selma kicked him hard in the back of the leg. He dropped to one knee, but hit her across the side of the head with the gun he was holding. Selma fell to the floor, unconscious.

Sharyn launched herself at him, their bodies rolling across the basement floor. She struck him with her elbow on the nose and he howled in pain, blood spurting from his face.

He punched her in the jaw with surprising strength for a man who wasn't known to do more than go from limousine to office on a regular basis. Sharyn felt sick and dizzy for a moment, still suffering from the effects of the blow to the head he'd greeted her with at the barn.

She could feel a gun between them. It was pressing into her sternum. She tried to get her hand around his on it. She knew right away it was her grandfather's revolver. She forced herself to focus. She couldn't lose this fight. She wouldn't die by the weapon that had protected her.

"Give up, Sharyn. You can't win against me. You never could. Come with me. We would make a great team."

"Not in this life."

"It doesn't have to be this way. Don't make me kill you."

She heard the sound of a low flying plane. It must be Jack's ride to Argentina. She knew he heard it too when he stopped fighting to keep the gun from her and listened. It was only an instant, but she took advantage of it.

He was leaning over her, using his weight to bear down on the gun to keep her from taking it. She let go with one hand and used her palm to strike him sharply in the throat. He coughed and choked, rolling away from her. She picked the gun up from her side and got to her feet.

Selma was trying to stand. Sharyn leaned down to help her aunt up off the cold floor and Selma yelled a warning. Sharyn turned quickly and saw Jack advancing on her with a large crowbar in his hand. His face was distorted into a grimace of anger and hatred.

He swung the crowbar at her, narrowly missing her head. She twisted to one side and caught him in her sights as he came back for another pass with the tool. The sound of her grandfather's revolver going off echoed through the basement around them that was filled with pieces of the Howard family history.

Sharyn thought she hit him, but he kept coming toward her with the crowbar. He swung again and she moved sharply away, firing into him two more times.

Jack dropped to his knees and stared at her. He threw the crowbar away and put his hand to his chest. When he looked at his fingers, they were covered in blood. "What have you done?"

Sharyn held the gun steady on him. She watched as he toppled forward, his face buried in old newspapers. She was prepared for him to move again. She wasn't ready to hear Selma's voice telling her it was over and urging her to put down the gun.

The door from the kitchen flew open and Ed, Terry, and Marvella ran down the stairs with their weapons drawn.

When Sharyn saw them, she knew it was all right. Her death grip on the revolver loosened and she slowly put it back into her holster.

Ed knelt beside Jack and checked his pulse. He shook his head. "He's not going anywhere."

Marvella helped Selma off the floor and asked if she needed an ambulance. Selma immediately ran upstairs to search for Sam with Marvella one step behind her.

Terry stepped in close to Sharyn and looked at the blood on her face and uniform. "Are you okay? Do you need the paramedics?"

"Don't bother asking her that. She'd never admit it if something was wrong." Ed took out his cell phone and called for help. "Let's all go upstairs and sort this out."

Sharyn tried to speak, but couldn't get past opening her mouth. Jack was dead. She killed him. Her head hurt and a faint trickle of blood welled up at the side of her mouth where he'd slapped her. She walked up the stairs behind Ed with Terry coming up after her as though he was afraid she might not make it to the kitchen.

She looked back once and saw Jack's crumpled body on the floor. She was afraid Ed was wrong and he was still alive. Panic seized her and she gripped her revolver. But he didn't move. It was hard to believe he was really dead, but logic came to her rescue and assured her that what Ed said was true.

Marvella and Selma found Sam upstairs, tied to one of the heavy oak chairs. He was halfway through the ropes Jack had used on him.

Selma cut his bonds with a sharp kitchen knife and Marvella helped him to his feet. "You're going to have a bad bruise there." Selma pointed to the side of his face where Jack had surprised him with a piece of firewood as he walked into the kitchen.

"I heard three shots." Sam looked at Sharyn. "Is he dead?"

She nodded, watching as Sam took Selma in his arms, examining the bruise forming on the side of her face. It was as well that she killed Jack. She knew from the look in Sam's eyes that he would have killed him if she hadn't.

It seemed to her that she was standing off from a great distance watching everyone in the kitchen as they tried to piece together what happened. She heard Selma explain that Jack attacked Sam then forced her into the basement. She tried to get out and tried to call for help, but nothing happened until Jack came back downstairs with Sharyn, unconscious, across his shoulders. Selma tried again to force her way out of the basement, but Jack was too strong. He closed them all down there and waited for Sharyn to wake up.

The sound of several sirens was steadily moving closer to the house. They were about half an hour out of

Diamond Springs. Probably the paramedic unit from the fire station on Main Street.

Sharyn logged those normal thoughts in her brain. She saw Ed look at her with concern in his usually laughing eyes. He wasn't laughing. He walked over to where she was standing beside the kitchen cabinet where she snitched cookies from Aunt Selma's cookie jar when she was a child. He put one hand on her shoulder and glanced behind her head.

She saw his mouth moving and heard him speaking, but it was distorted. She didn't know what he was saying. She felt herself slowly sinking down toward the floor. Everyone in the room was looking at her. She tried to speak and reassure them, but she couldn't find the words. Blackness surrounded her along with Jack's voice asking her what she'd done.

"Get in here!" Ed yelled to the paramedics who showed up at the door. "What took you so long? We've got injured people here."

Terry had lifted Sharyn in his arms with a look of devastation on his lean, young face.

"Is she shot?" the lead paramedic asked Ed.

"I don't know. That's why you're here. She seemed fine one minute then she was on the floor. There's blood all over her."

The paramedics took over. Two more units responded as the first unit took Sharyn's inert body from

Terry and put her on a stretcher. Nick and Ernie drove up in time to see the ambulance doors close and the first unit head back toward town.

Terry and Ed were already running toward their car. Ernie glanced at their faces and put one hand on Nick's arm. "What happened? Is Sharyn . . . ?"

"I don't know," Ed yelled. "They're taking her in now. Jack's dead. She killed him. Selma and Sam are inside. I think they're okay."

Ernie nodded and glanced at where Nick had been standing. He was gone. He was already running back to the SUV. Ernie grabbed the door as the engine started. "She's okay. I *know* she's okay."

Nick gunned the powerful engine, racing up the long driveway toward the road. "She better be. He can only die once."

The room was quiet and cool when Sharyn woke up again. She wasn't sure where she was. It smelled a little musty, like old books and clothes. Everything felt damp, but it wasn't raining. She was confused and a little scared.

She glanced around the room. The lights were turned down low. She could make out forms like furniture, but that was all. She was in a bed, a small light on a table beside her. There were curtains around the bed. She realized she was in a hospital.

"How are you feeling? That was quite a bump on the head you took," a familiar voice said.

"I don't know. How long have I been out?"

"Not long. Don't worry." Jack's face came into the light beside her. "I've been watching over you."

Sharyn sat up in bed, gasping for breath and fighting with the sheet and blanket covering her. Her heart was pounding as she pushed aside the last wispy threads of unconsciousness.

"Take it easy." Nick got up from a chair beside the bed. "It took all the king's horses and all the king's men to put that head back together. Let's not make it worse again."

"Jack." The name tore from her throat. "He's dead?"

"Undeniably." He squeezed her hand. "If you like, you can help me do the autopsy. That always convinces people that someone is dead."

She sat back against the pillows and stared at Nick. "Could you turn the lights on? All of them."

He walked to the door and turned on the overhead light. "Nightmares?"

"Only the one." She didn't enlighten him. "What time is it?"

"About two A.M. Selma is fine. Sam is fine. Diamond Springs and the rest of the world is safe for the moment. Even Supergirl gets to rest sometimes. The doctor says this is *your* time."

Sharyn felt better than she had at the farmhouse. She drank some water he held for her and smiled. "I think it's going to be okay now."

"I don't know about that. You stood me up for our re-union date and then I had to come to the hospital when I wasn't working. A thing like that takes its toll on a man. I don't think we can date anymore."

Sharyn nodded, sorry afterward because it hurt her head. "What did you have in mind?"

Nick perched on the side of the bed, and held her hand again. "I think we have to get married. There's no other way this will work. Especially with both of us getting kicked around by criminals. The insurance will be better and no one can ask me if I'm your next of kin."

Surprised, she smiled. "I suppose that might work. My mother loves weddings."

"What's not to love? Too much food. Too much to drink. I hear the Stag Inn Doe is doing receptions now. That would be perfect."

"If you say so. I was thinking about that overlook on Diamond Mountain. That would be a perfect place to get married."

He kissed her lightly and smiled into her eyes. "Only if you're an eagle. We'll have to compromise."

"We'll *always* have to compromise."

"True," he agreed. "I love you anyway. I wouldn't want to compromise myself with anyone but you."

She leaned forward slightly until her lips met his. "Me either. I love you too. How long until I get out of here?"

Epilogue

DIAMOND SPRINGS GAZETTE WEDDING NOTES

Sheriff and Medical Examiner Tie Knot

Sheriff Sharyn Howard married Montgomery County Medical Examiner Nick Thomopolis on a quiet Friday evening when all of her deputies could spend at least a few minutes at the reception afterward. The entire affair was held in April at the Howard family homestead. Most of it was outside with the bees buzzing and the smell of honeysuckle accompanying laughter and accordion music provided by tracker Doody Franklin and a few of his dogs.

Most of Diamond Springs and the rest of the county managed to drop by at one time or another. The bride was given in marriage by lead Mont-

gomery County Deputy, Ernie Watkins. Her maid of honor was her aunt, Selma Howard-Two-Rivers who looked radiant in a floor-length peach-colored dress. Other bridesmaids included the sheriff's sister, Kristie Howard, Deputies Marvella Honeycutt and Cari Long, and newly reinstated attorney, Jill Madison-Farmer.

The bride wore a floor-length white gown embroidered with seed pearls and a long white veil. Her pearl necklace was an heirloom handed down from her great grandmother. Her bright red hair shone in the sunshine like a new copper penny.

Her mother, Faye Howard-Talbot was also present with ex-senator Caison Talbot. She wore blue brocade with a blue feathered hat.

The couple plan to take a honeymoon cruise to Jamaica.